450

The Popsicle Journal

Also by Don Trembath

Harper Winslow series

The Tuesday Cafe
A Fly Named Alfred
A Beautiful Place on Yonge Street

More teen fiction

Lefty Carmichael Has A Fit

The Black Belt Series

Frog Face and the Three Boys
One Missing Finger

The Popsicle Journal

Don Trembath

ORCA BOOK PUBLISHERS

National Library of Canada Cataloguing in Publication Data

Trembath, Don, 1963–
    The popsicle journal

    ISBN 1-55143-185-8

    I. Title.
PS8589.R392P66 2001   jC813'.54   C2001-910950-4
PZ7.T1925Po 2001

Library of Congress Catalog Card Number: 2001092683

Orca Book Publishers gratefully acknowledges the support of our publishing programs provided by the following agencies: the Department of Canadian Heritage, The Canada Council for the Arts, and the British Columbia Arts Council.

Cover design by Christine Toller
Cover illustration by Ron Lightburn/Limner Imagery
Printed and bound in Canada

Orca Book Publishers
PO Box 5626, Station B
Victoria, BC V8R 6S4
Canada

Orca Book Publishers
PO Box 468
Custer, WA 98240-0468
USA

03 02 01 • 5 4 3 2 1

To my charming niece, Stephanie,
because she likes Harper.

< 1 >

Before I get into anything else, I want to tell you about this job I have.

I'm a reporter with a newspaper called *The Emville Express*. I work every day after school and on weekends. I cover sports I know nothing about, interview people I've never seen before, and take pictures with a camera that sat collecting dust in my closet for five years.

And you know what? I'm good at it. I meet all my deadlines. I've learned how to develop my own film in the darkroom. I can add two paragraphs to a story at the last minute, or decide which two have to go, if we have to rearrange a page for a new advertisement.

My editor said I'm the best student he's ever hired, and he's gone through fourteen of them in the last two years. "Harper," he said, "for a kid in grade eleven, you're doing a pretty good job."

I told him "Thank you very much" when he said that because I learned a long time ago to accept compliments when you get them. Then he said, "Now don't screw up," which is a little bit more in line with the way he usually talks.

His name is Kip Kelly. He's twenty-eight years old and has a grade ten education. He chews gum with his mouth open and walks around the office with a cigarette behind his ear the way a carpenter keeps a pencil. He shows up at work every morning with his sleeves rolled up past his elbows and his tie loose around his neck, as if he was coming off a tough twelve-hour shift, instead of just starting one.

He keeps a bottle of whisky in a drawer in his office. I know this because he pulled it out the day he hired me and had a drink with his office assistant, Dixie, who seemed more happy about the occasion than even I was.

Dixie is very small and thin and has billowy blonde hair that looks like a big, soft cloud resting on her head. She is about forty-five years old and wears more make-up than a clown working a birthday party. When she gets mad, like at a customer for refusing to pay a bill, or at the printer for messing up another ad, she throws things. On my first day, I walked in the front door and was nearly hit in the head by a flying stapler that left a tiny dent in the wall beside a plaque honoring her for community involvement as a Big Sister.

At other times over the past three weeks, which is how long I've been here, I have seen rulers, pencils, pens, erasers, and a box of paper clips (that opened in mid-flight) go whistling across the room; an ashtray bash against the photocopier; a pack of gum bounce off the back of Kip's head; and, after a call from her ex-boyfriend, the coffee pot (it was empty, but it still made a mess) smashed to smithereens against Tom's desk.

She also smokes, swears, wears jeans that would fit a skinny twelve year old, and flirts with pretty well every male who walks through the front door, which is why I told Dad to come in through the back if he ever decides to drop by to see me.

Tom Davey is the ad salesman. He has tightly curled hair that clings to his head like moss on a rock, and he stands six feet, four inches tall and weighs 246 pounds. He is a bodybuilder. He eats a head of lettuce in his hand like it's a green apple, and he has a small fridge by his desk and a miniature microwave oven on the counter near the darkroom for his food. He eats eighteen egg whites a day, and six cans of tuna. He can tell you from memory how much protein is in ten ounces of chicken breasts, and the amount of carbohydrates in a processed cheese slice, which he never eats, unless it's a fat-free cheese slice and he's short on calories.

His favorite hockey team is the Philadelphia Flyers. In particular, the Flyers of the '70s, when they won all of their Stanley Cups.

Don't ask me why I know this. I do not come from a very sports-minded family. I come from a hard-working family. A dedicated, committed, loyal, respected family that regards reading books and playing sports as leisure activities that, quite simply, to quote Mom, "we don't have time for." We also don't talk very much with each other, or share things, and we spend a lot of time creating the impression that around our place, everything is just as it seems, meaning everything is perfect, which is why, when I started a fire in my school last year and ended up in court, it created quite a stir around our kitchen table.

I was charged with causing property damage under $500 and ordered by a judge to write an essay on how I was going to turn my life around. To help me out, Mom enrolled me in a writing class called The Tuesday Cafe, which proved to be quite exciting, and a little weird, especially at the start. It was the first time in my life that I was actually encouraged to write, and I did pretty well at it. So well in fact that I got a job at the school newspaper after my essay was completed.

I wrote a column called "Fly On The Wall."

It was the coolest thing in the whole paper until someone threatened to kill me.

But anyway. I have one brother and one sister. They are both way older than me and we have almost nothing in common, other than the fact that we share the same parents, apparently.

My dad has been a family doctor in Emville for over thirty years, and a town councilor for nearly as long. His name is Benjamin Winslow. He has been a Volunteer Of The Year twice and a Citizen Of The Year once. The only person who has won these honors more times than he has is my mom, Judy Winslow, who has also been a Volunteer Of The Year twice, but has won the Citizen Of The Year three times, which has got to be a record, for if there was anyone out there in any town who had won the award more times than that, then he or she would be completely and totally insufferable, and therefore hard to vote for. As it is right now, Mom is only approaching insufferable, which is bad enough, but she is still manageable to live with.

Of course, Tom knew none of this when he walked over and told me that he liked the Philadelphia Flyers. He had a half-eaten cucumber the size of a fire log in his hand, and he said, "So, you're the new sports guy, eh?"

I remember shrugging my shoulders. "I guess so," I said, without enthusiasm. It was true that sports was one of the areas I would be covering, but by no means did I consider myself to be an actual sports reporter, nor do I today.

"Well, I don't think my Flyers are gonna do it this year," he said, as if I had asked him.

"Your who?" I said. This was before I knew exactly what the Flyers were.

"My Flyers. I don't see them getting it done this year. Too many holes to fill. Too many questions without answers." He shook his head. I could tell this was an upsetting revelation for him. "Bring back the glory days, that's all I have to say. Freddie the Fog. The Hammer. Moose Dupont. Hound Dog Kelly."

"Are these people?" I said, not meaning to be rude.

It was right there that Tom lost whatever respect he ever had for me, and probably a fair bit of what he had for Kip, because it was to Kip's office that he went next, after leaving my work area without saying another word. I could hear the two of them getting pretty loud in there, and when Tom came out, Kip called me over and told me to go easy on the big lug, explaining that as unbelievably huge and muscular as he may be, Tom was still a pretty sensitive guy, especially when it came to sports.

It was also the one and only time that Tom has ever

initiated a conversation with me, even though our desks are only about ten feet apart.

The first story I wrote was about a couple celebrating their seventieth wedding anniversary.

Their names were Horace and Gertie Schotz, and they lived in Room 102 of the Forest Grove Manor For Retired Living right here in Emville. Horace was ninety-four years old and Gertie was ninety-one.

Kip sent me over the day after he hired me.

My interview with them did not produce the most scintillating piece of journalism ever recorded, especially since Gertie spent the entire time in bed with an icepack on her head, moaning about a headache, and Horace kept confusing me with his grandson. He asked me three times how the new tractor was treating me, and when I finally convinced him that I didn't have a tractor, he asked me what the hell was I doing living on a farm without one.

Besides that, everything went okay. A woman named Patsy was there to help me. She was the Activities Coordinator who had called us about the anniversary celebration in the first place. She told me all about Horace and Gertie and how they had met and what they had done with their lives.

I made notes of everything she said and wrote the story as soon as I returned to the office. Before I could finish, Dixie came by and read it over my shoulder.

She liked it, which wasn't a complete surprise. When she wasn't winging things around the office, or cursing a blue streak at some numbskull on the telephone, which was pretty well anybody, including Kip when he was out covering a story, and me, eventually, after we got to know each other, she could be quite a compassionate person. Actually, when it came to anything to do with romance, as in the story of Gertie and Horace, she could become a blubbering, sniffing, make-up-smearing mess.

"That is such a good story, Harper," she said, dabbing her eyes with a Kleenex and hiccuping in my ear. "Kip's gonna hate it."

I stopped typing and looked at her. "He's gonna what?"

She smiled and patted me on the shoulder. "Don't worry. I'll take care of it."

She did, too.

At the end of my first week, I was called into his office and told to shut the door.

Kip was sitting behind his desk, leaning back in his chair, his hands behind his head like a sunbather, his mouth smacking away at a new piece of gum. Or at least, I assumed it was a new piece. Newer than the piece he had in his mouth the day before, anyway.

He had a copy of *The Baseball News* spread out on his desk.

Kip was a baseball freak, I was soon to discover, and just about every time he opened his mouth to talk, something about baseball came out of it.

He asked me how I thought things were going and I told him fine. Then he said, "Dixie tells me you're a wizard at your computer." I shrugged my shoulders and said that I wasn't so sure about that.

Unfortunately, he agreed with me.

"I think your writing could use a little toughening up, myself," he said. He had a very unnerving habit of staring right into your eyes whenever he spoke.

"A little what?" I said, my face turning instantly red. I was not exactly thick-skinned when it came to dealing with criticism.

"A little toughening up. It needs a little zing. A little ouch. A little Nolan Ryan. You know who Nolan Ryan is?"

I had to think for a minute. "Nolan who?"

"Ryan."

I shook my head. "No, I don't."

"How about Randy Johnson?"

"No."

"Pedro Martinez?"

"No."

"You ever watch a baseball game in your life?"

I shrugged my shoulders. "Maybe one."

"One?" he said, a look of disbelief on his face.

"Or two," I said, padding my numbers.

He tried a different approach. "Alright. Well, you know who the pitcher is at least?"

"Yes."

"Who is he?"

"He's the guy who throws the ball."

He nodded. "Perfect. He's the guy who throws the ball. And some guys throw the ball harder than other guys. That's where Nolan Ryan comes in. And Randy Johnson. And Roger Clemens."

A light went on in my head. "I know him," I said, sounding more excited than I wanted to.

"Who?"

"Roger Clemens."

"How do you know him?"

"My girlfriend likes him."

Kip started to look impressed. "You have a girlfriend?"

"Yes."

"And she likes baseball?"

"She loves it."

His face brightened, as if his decision to hire me was a good one after all. "Well, good for her."

"Unfortunately, she lives in Toronto," I said.

Kip shrugged. To him, where Sunny lived didn't matter. "Well, the next time you talk to her, ask her if she knows these guys. Martinez and Johnson and guys like that. If she does, get her to tell you all about them, because that's how I want you to write. Like a strike-out king."

"Like a what?"

He shook his head. "Forget it. I've got something else I want to tell you about."

I braced myself for more sports talk.

"I'm handing over my column space to you."

I sat up straight in my chair. "You're what?"

"It's Dixie's idea. She thinks it'll give me more time for my editorials, and with an election coming up, I'm gonna need it."

I was stunned. "My own column space?"

"It'll run every week, on the page opposite my stuff. Keep it light. Make it good. And make sure it's on my desk every Friday morning at ten o'clock sharp."

This was too good to be true.

"And next week, we start the election campaign. Nomination papers are due on Wednesday, and this year's gonna be a knockout. I can feel it. So be ready."

I thanked him and walked out of his office in a cloud. One week on the job and I was already a columnist. Alright, a fill-in, substitute columnist, but still … I didn't touch down until I talked to my good friend Billy on the phone, who told me what to name my new column and gave me an idea what I should write about.

‹ 2 ›

"The Popsicle Journal" was the name Billy came up with. He suggested it right away and stuck with it until I gave in.

Billy is a friend of mine I met at The Tuesday Cafe. He's older than me by twelve years. He doesn't work because of all the medication he's on. Mom calls him the sweetest, most innocent person she's ever met.

He lives his life a wee bit different from most people I know. Last summer he wore his bathing suit every week to the church he goes to because there was a brand new waterpark across the street. When I asked him why he didn't just bring a change of clothes, he said, "And then what, crumple up my tie into a little ball and stuff it in a bag? Forget it. You can't iron those things. Not if you don't have an iron."

"Aren't you a little embarrassed though, sitting in a church in your bathing suit?" I said. I sure would have been, I can tell you that.

He gave me a look like I was crazy. "I'm not talking about my Speedo. I save that for lane swimming on

Thursday nights, after bowling. I'm talking about my boxers. My long orange boxer shorts. And no. I'm not a little embarrassed. I'm proud of my physique. I do push-ups."

I let it go after that. I didn't have the nerve to ask him if he actually wore his Speedo into the bowling alley, or changed when he got to the pool.

Some people think he's a nutcase, but I've never been one of them. Besides, I don't exactly have a long list of people phoning me every night, asking me to movies and parties and everything.

Billy has a new girlfriend named Carmela, who was at his apartment when I called him.

Carmela is short and pudgy and has thick black hair and a permanently bright smile on her face. She is the biggest KISS fan on earth and is an amazing trivia buff when it comes to music.

"Quick, ask me a question about music," she said the first time I met her. I had run into them at a McDonald's, where Billy was trying to teach her how to memorize the ingredients of a Big Mac.

"Two all-beef patties," he started off saying.

"Two all-beef patties," said Carmela, rolling her eyes behind her glasses and stuffing a few of his fries into her mouth.

"Special sauce."

She looked at him. "That's not special sauce."

"Special sauce," said Billy, with a nod.

"That is not special sauce," said Carmela, shaking her head. "There is nothing special there. Nothing at all."

"Special sauce," said Billy again, sticking with the program.

"No way."

"Special sauce," said Billy, letting her know that he wasn't going to stop.

"Alright. Special sauce. Brother."

"Lettuce, cheese, pickles."

Carmela looked at him again. "I can't do all that."

"Lettuce, cheese, pickles."

"Forget it. I'm not doing that."

Billy hesitated. Then he said, slowly, "Lettuce."

"No," said Carmela. "It isn't real lettuce anyway. It's some kind of fake stuff. My rabbit wouldn't go near it, and that's all she eats — lettuce, carrots, and apple-skins."

"Lettuce," said Billy again, like a robot.

It was right there when I said hi to them. Billy dropped the lesson in Food Science and introduced us. Then Carmela asked me to ask her a question.

I don't listen to music that much, so I didn't really know anything to ask her.

"Ask me to name all the members of the rock band KISS," she said, as a suggestion.

"Alright. Name all the members of the rock band KISS."

She named them, one after the other, as if they were her brothers. "Ace Frehley, Paul Stanley, Gene Simmons, he's the one with the long tongue that he sticks out all the time, like this — BLAH!, and Peter Criss. He's the drummer. He sings the song 'Beth.' It's the most beautiful song in the world. I cry every time I hear it. And they're a rock band. They don't even sing that kind of music."

I heard Billy tell her my news about getting my own column. I was sure she'd be excited. She knows I want to be a writer, and I had told her myself that I had gotten the job at the paper.

I waited to hear her response, but instead, all I heard was Billy telling her again. And again, only slower this time. And once more after that. Finally I cut in and said, "Billy, what's the problem over there?"

My patience could wear a little thin sometimes, especially when I was excited.

"She can't hear me," said Billy.

"She can't hear you?" I said. That didn't make any sense. Billy's apartment is tiny, and the two of them almost always sit together in the living room, on the couch, watching old movies or doing large-print crossword puzzles and word searches. "Why not?"

"She's wearing her headphones," said Billy.

I rolled my eyes. "So, why are you telling her if she's wearing headphones?"

"She wants to know," said Billy.

"She wants to know what? How does she even know who you're talking to?"

"I told her."

"How?"

"She read my lips. I mouthed the word Harper and she knew right away. Then she said, 'What does he want?' and I read her lips so I would know what she was talking about, and then I told her. But she couldn't understand me so I told her again. But she still couldn't understand me so I told her again."

"Okay, Billy," I said, rubbing my forehead. "I get the picture."

"But then she still couldn't understand me so I had

to tell her again."

"Okay, Billy. Forget it."

"I don't have to forget it. This time she got it."

I shook my head. "Well, good for her," I said.

"It usually doesn't take her this long, though," said Billy. "There must be something wrong. She's usually pretty good reading lips."

"How does a person become pretty good reading lips when they're not deaf?" I said. I know this had nothing to do with what I was calling him about, but he had me going on it.

"We practice."

"You what?"

"We practice. All the time."

"Why?"

"Why not?"

"Why not? Who practices reading lips when you don't have to?"

"We do," said Billy.

"Why?"

"Why not? It breaks the monotony of just talking back and forth all the time."

I closed my eyes. You would think, after all the experience I have talking with him, that I would be able to avoid conversations like this, and sometimes I can, but not always. "Why don't you just change the subject?" I said.

"To what?"

"To anything."

"Well, this way it doesn't matter what we're talking about because we always have to figure out what each one of us is saying."

I could feel a dull pain developing in my head. So I took action and changed the subject. I asked him if he had any suggestions for a name for my column. He said The Popsicle Journal.

"But that's your name, Billy," I said. A couple of years ago, he had started a little newspaper at The Cafe and he had called it The Popsicle Journal. I don't think it actually ever went anywhere, but still, I was a little uncomfortable just taking something that was already his.

"Not anymore it's not," he said. "I'm selling it to you."

"You're selling it?" I said. This was a surprise. I had never considered Billy to be a businessman before.

"Name your price."

I hesitated. "You want me to name the price?"

"It's your column."

"But it's your name."

"Not anymore it's not."

"Well, you haven't sold it to me yet."

"I'm just waiting for a price. The rest of the deal is done."

I had to think. I had no idea how much to offer Billy for his name. I didn't even know if I wanted it. "I don't know, Billy."

"Well think about it. You can pay me tomorrow. Or the day after. I'll be around. I have no out-of-town-business to take care of. You know where I live."

"I don't even know if I want that name, though. What's it mean? What's the point of it?"

"Just a minute," he said. "Carmela wants an update."

I sat back in my chair and listened to him talk to Carmela again, or whatever it is you call it when one person is talking and the other person is intentionally not listening to the words.

Finally, and to my surprise, because it seemed that she was quite into her music, she picked up the phone.

"Harper," she said, "Billy tells me you don't want to use his name."

The two of them had met at a floor hockey tryout for the Special Olympics. Carmela was trying out for goal and Billy was playing center. They both made the team, although Billy is now the starting goalie, and she's the leading scorer.

"Not exactly," I said. "I said I wasn't sure."

"Well, here's what I think," said Carmela. Like Billy, she is not the fastest person on earth when it comes to thinking, and she lives in a group home for people with disabilities, but she knows him very well, and she is a great communicator when she takes her headphones off. "I think you should use it because Billy can't use it anymore."

"Why can't Billy use it anymore?" I said.

"Because he's done with it. He's finished. He's taken it as far as it will go. That paper of his is dead. Besides, think about it. It's the perfect name for a newspaper column. The Popsicle Journal. It's cool. It's light. It's refreshing. And when you're done with it, you can throw it in the garbage. What could be better than that?"

I thought for a moment before answering. I think what she was saying was that I could use the name as a way of continuing Billy's idea of creating something that was a treat to read, just as a Popsicle is a treat to eat. As for the throwaway part, well, she was probably right about that, too, although in today's environmentally correct world, people recycled things like newspapers and tiny wooden Popsicle sticks.

"Okay," I said, with a nod, even though I knew she couldn't see it.

"Okay what?" said Carmela.

"Okay, I'll go with it. I'll go with The Popsicle Journal."

"You will?"

"Sure. Why not? It's an excellent idea."

She passed the phone to Billy and told him my decision.

"Well, well, well," said Billy. "So you've come to your senses."

"I'd never lost track of my senses, Billy."

"I'm not so sure about that."

"Well, I didn't," I said. "But thanks for the name. I'll use it wisely."

"You better," he said, sounding like my dad. "Popsicles melt, you know. You leave them out there in the heat for too long, you'll end up with an arm full of Kool-Aid and a stain on your shirt. And with your mom, that would not go over very well."

"I'll be careful," I said, and I hung up before Carmela could plug in her headphones again.

< 3 >

The only other person who works at the paper on a regular basis is Paula. She is Kip's editorial assistant. She graduated from high school last year. She is also the sister of the woman he used to go out with.

Paula is eighteen years old, but she acts like she's about forty, although I'm not completely sure about that, since I don't hang around with too many forty year olds.

She has plain, straight brown hair that hangs in the front to just above her eyes. She wears glasses. She's heavy, or, as Mom would put it, she's about three times bigger than she has to be.

But the most defining characteristic about Paula is, she's nice. She is an exceptionally nice person. In fact, she's the nicest person I've ever met, by far. She's like a dog that won't stop licking your face, or a cat that keeps purring and rubbing against your leg until you're ready to grab it by the tail and wing it outside. Not that I've ever had a cat before. Mom does not like the hair they leave behind on the couch, and once, when I was about seven and we were at a Christmas party, she saw a big fluffy gray one sniffing and licking the turkey as it cooled on the counter, and she almost got sick.

She spent the whole rest of the night shaking her head and washing her hands. And she didn't eat a bit of food.

I met Paula on my third day. I was working on a story about a fundraising drive in town for a new recreation center, and she walked up to my desk and said, "I'm sorry. I haven't had the privilege of meeting you yet. I'm Paula, Kip's editorial assistant."

Now I don't know about anyone else, but that is sure not the way I introduce myself to new people. I usually just walk up to them and say, "Hi. My name's Harper," or something clever like that. And I don't do it very often, either.

"Hi," I said, looking up from my computer. "I'm Harper."

Paula smiled, as if to say that she already knew that. "Oh, I already know that. You're the fabulous new writer we have in our office."

I started to blush again, but I didn't have a chance to say anything, which was good, because I'm not exactly rehearsed when it comes to responding to someone who calls me fabulous.

"Now, is there anything I can get for you? A coffee? Tea? Anything from across the street?"

"No, thanks," I said.

"They have these lovely little ice-cream bars there that are just so delicious. Of course they're full of fat, or so Tom tells me. He reads the labels on all these things I bring in. I never bother. I don't have the time. Well, actually, I don't have the willpower. I don't want to know what's inside the little devils. I just wanna eat them. But is there anything I can get you?"

The second most defining feature about Paula is she tends to talk a lot.

"No, thanks," I said, again, as politely as I could. I threw in a smile this time, for good measure. I was right into the story I was doing, and Kip wanted it done before I went home. And I was also feeling a little put off by her niceness: in the back of my mind I was starting to wonder what she was up to, which probably says more about me than it does about her, but still, it's the truth.

"Well, you let me know if you change your mind," she said.

"I will."

"Now I can see you're busy, so I won't bother you anymore, but you let me know. I'll be right over here." She pointed towards the corner where her office was. "I'll be waiting."

I smiled again, and nodded, and watched as she went into her office. Then, before I could return to my story, she popped back out again.

"What about hot chocolate?" she said, poking her head around the door frame. "You probably don't even drink coffee."

"No, I don't, actually," I said.

"Well, for goodness sakes, then," she said. "Let's get you a hot chocolate." She started marching towards the little coffee area in the far corner.

"No, thanks," I said again, but I was too late. She had a packet of hot chocolate in her hand, and she had already plugged in the kettle.

"We'll call it a toast in your honor," she said. "Harper's Hot Chocolate."

"It's really not necessary," I said.

Paula turned and gave me a big, stern smile. "I know that. I know it's not necessary. It's not painful, either. So just let me do it, and enjoy it, and then you can have all the quiet time you want."

She was the same way the next week, although this time, I needed it.

Kip called me into his office the second I arrived from school and told me to sit down. I could tell by the tone of his voice that he was not about to offer me an even greater amount of space for my column, or the keys to his car for the weekend.

I sat down in the chair.

He walked over to his desk and picked up a manila envelope. "I got the nomination papers from the town office today. We've got nine candidates running for five councilor positions."

"That sounds good," I said, figuring that it must be good, since nine didn't go into five very well, which made for a healthy bit of competition.

"And we have three candidates for mayor."

I nodded. That sounded fine too. But I knew he hadn't called me in just to share this with me.

Kip dropped the envelope on his desk. "I see one of them is your father."

I was not surprised to hear this. Dad had told Mom and me about his intentions to run for mayor just after school started. "I know," I said, with a nod. "He told me he was going to."

Kip stared at me for a moment. "So, you knew that," he said.

"Yes."

He walked around his desk and sat down. "When did you find out?"

I thought for a moment. "Maybe a month ago. He took my mom and me out for supper."

"How nice," said Kip, without meaning it.

"It was, actually," I said.

"And what exactly did he say?"

"He said he was going to run for mayor."

"And what did he tell you about telling other people?"

"He said he wanted to keep it quiet so he could get a team together. An election team."

Kip nodded. "And you listened to him."

"Sure," I said, with a shrug. What could be so wrong with that?

Kip thought for a moment and blew a couple of bubbles with his gum.

"Do you know what a scoop is, Harper?" he said after a moment.

"A scoop?"

"As it relates to the newspaper business. Yes. A scoop."

"Not really."

"No?"

"No. I mean, I know it's got something to do with getting a story, but I don't know much more than that."

He started to chew even harder. "A scoop is when you get a story before anyone else does. It's when the other newspapers in town pick up your paper and say,

'Damnit! Why didn't we know about that?'"

"Okay," I said. I was still not catching on to what the problem was, although I knew there was a problem and that I had something to do with it.

"They are very hard to come by," he said, staring into my eyes. "I get very happy when we get one. And very upset when we get scooped. But you know what really drives me nuts?"

I shook my head.

"When we have a scoop right before our eyes, and we miss it. That drives me crazy. You know why?"

I gulped. I had a feeling this is where I came in. "Why?"

"Because it's a missed chance to rattle the friggin' cages of all those hotshot politicians who think they know so much. It's a chance for us to actually do our job and deliver real news to the people out there, instead of the stuff that guys like your dad want us to print, when they want us to print it. That's why."

I sat motionless in my chair. All of a sudden I knew what this was about.

"Now if we had run a story a week ago about your dad's decision to run for mayor, we would have scooped that other rag in town, and we would have really stirred things up around here. Maybe somebody else would have decided to run against him. Maybe old man Harrison would have run again."

I perked up when I heard this. "He already told my dad he wasn't going to. That's why Dad's running."

"Oh, really," said Kip.

"Yes. He said that to my dad."

Kip stared at me for a moment. "Well, you know what, Harper? Politicians lie. Not all the time, and not every single one of them, but they do. They lie. Just like you and I do. Just like Dixie and Tom do. They bend the truth. They manipulate the facts. They forget to tell you things. They remember to not tell you things. And when you ask them about it later, they either deny it, or they say, 'Oh, I'm sorry. I made a mistake,' because whatever it was they were lying about is over with and they don't have to worry about it anymore."

I sat without speaking.

"But that's not what your dad did to you. Don't worry. I'm not saying he lied to you. But he did pull a fast one on you."

"No, he didn't," I said. I could feel my blood starting to boil.

"Of course he did."

"No, he didn't."

Kip's face began to harden. "He told you not to tell anybody, even though he knew that, as a reporter, it's your job to report the news, whether he wants you to or not. And your dad deciding to run for mayor is news. In this town, it's major news."

"He told me that before I got this job," I said, as if it made a difference.

"So what?"

"So when he told me, I was just his son, Harper the high school student. I wasn't working for any newspaper."

"Do you think it crossed his mind when you got the job at the newspaper that his decision to run for mayor would be newsworthy?"

"I don't know. But even if it did, that's not pulling a fast one on me."

"Sure it is."

"No it's not."

"Of course it is. He knows this business better than I do. He's been a politician for as long as he's been a doctor. He handles reporters like we're a bunch of newborn babies. And you know something else? I saw him at Ruby's just the other day, having lunch, and I walked over and asked him, very casually, if he was thinking of running for mayor, because you know, he's been around for a long time and people have always said he'd make a good one. You know what he said to me? He said he hadn't even considered it. His plate was already too full. I remember those words very clearly because as soon as he said them, his lunch arrived, this great big plate of salad and some kind of sandwich, and he looked at me said, 'See what I mean?' and we both had a big laugh. Ha, ha, ha. Very funny. And now this. The joke's on us again. That's what I call pulling a fast one."

I could think of nothing to say. But Kip was right, and in my rapidly sinking heart, I knew it.

"Now keep your eyes open and your head up. And the next time your dad tells you something he doesn't want anyone else to hear, pull out your notepad and write it down."

I remained quiet.

"Now go see Tom. He's got some business feature he wants you to do."

I left his office and walked over to my desk. Tom was on the phone so I just sat down and waited. My mind was numb. I felt like I had just been laid out on the street and run over by about fifty gravel trucks. But that wasn't the worst of it. The worst of it was, I didn't feel like a reporter anymore. I felt like a pretender, or an actor trying to look the part instead of actually being the part, and I was even doing a lousy job of that, too.

A good reporter recognizes a story the second it happens. A very good reporter sees the story coming and writes about it before it even arrives, or is standing there waiting for it when it does arrive.

There is no name for a reporter who lives and eats breakfast and goes out for supper with a news story for over a month and doesn't even know it's there.

I felt like someone who shouldn't even be delivering the papers, much less writing in them. The business feature I was waiting to hear about didn't make me feel any better. Business features were glorified advertisements. They weren't about news. They were about selling shoes or new homes or fancy new fitness equipment.

Anybody could write a business feature.

I was just on the verge of becoming seriously depressed when my friend Paula suddenly appeared and asked if I wanted anything from across the street again.

My initial reaction was to say, sure, how about a job? Maybe I could sell ice-cream bars to nice fat people for the rest of my life.

But instead, I shook my head and mumbled a timid little "No thanks," since my big, muscular way of saying no had been blasted out of me by Kip.

"Are you sure?" she said.

I nodded. "Positive."

"How about some Cheezies? Do you like Cheezies?"

I looked at her. There was something about her that was definitely getting on my nerves.

"Or Pringles?" she said, before I could actually give her an answer about the Cheezies.

"No," I said, keeping it simple.

"Oh, I love Pringles. I eat a whole tube watching *Survivor* every Thursday night. I spend the whole time wondering how I could smuggle the stupid things onto that island they're on."

Wow, that's very interesting, I felt like saying. Tell me more, so Kip can come out of his office and see me sitting here doing nothing and get mad at me again.

"What about licorice? Everybody likes licorice."

"No, thanks," I said, again, this time with a bit more force than the first.

"Oh, come on. A string of red licorice? You're telling me a string of red licorice wouldn't do it for you right now? I loved that piece you did on the fundraising drive, by the way. I proofed it this afternoon."

I perked up slightly.

"I thought the way you pulled it all together was amazing. You did a super job. I just made a few changes to it, but that's all. Nothing major. Just a few little tweaks. You'll recognize it when you see it in the paper. Don't worry."

I nodded again and managed a smile. It was really just a simple little story about a group of people who had organized bottle drives and bingos as a way of contributing to a new recreation hall. I didn't think it was anything special. But at the same time, I could feel her words having an effect on me, like warm chicken soup when you have a cold. They were something I needed to hear.

"I think those people you talked to will be very happy when they see it. You're giving great recognition to their efforts."

I started to think about it a little more. I talked to four people and gave them all equal space in the piece. A couple of them gave me good quotes, like the one old guy who said, "That hall we have now, I remember walking into it when I was fifteen years old, we were throwing a party for my grandfather, and my dad looked around the inside of it and said to me, 'With a little sprucing up, this place could look like new again.' That was sixty-three years ago. Sixty-three years ago my father said that, and I'll bet they haven't put a new coat of paint on the place since."

I actually started the story with that. I wrote, "*Elmer Norton has many memories of the old recreation hall. Some of them good, some of them bad. But, as he puts it, like the hall itself, all of them are old.*"

"I see it as a page two or page three story, depending on how the election coverage goes," said Paula. "It's just starting, so there shouldn't be too many stories yet."

"Page two?" I said. A page two story and a column in the same paper?

"I think so," said Paula. "I'll talk to Kip about it. But page two should work. I don't see anything else going there."

I suddenly began to feel better. Not like a million dollars or anything, but at least I could raise my head again and look around the office like I deserved to be there.

"So, do you want a licorice?" said Paula, one more time. She was persistent, I can tell you that.

This time, I said yes. "I guess so. Sure," I said, and I smiled a genuine smile at her for making me feel better. Then I got up, and we walked over to the store together.

< 4 >

...or not, I was still ticked off at being duped by ... when I went home after work that night, I had ...ntention of telling him that until the election was ...e was a politician and I was a reporter, and that ...d be the nature of our relationship.

I didn't know exactly what that meant, mind you. ...ut I was pretty sure I could figure it out.

As soon as I walked in the door, however, I had to change my plan: my sister Clarissa was sitting alone in the kitchen with a glass of vodka in her hand and the bottle on the table in front of her.

This was a surprising scene for several reasons. For one, my sister doesn't live at home anymore. She lives in Edmonton with her husband, Michael, and their two kids. Two, not only does she not live here anymore, but she almost never visits here either, unless it's a very happy occasion, like a birthday celebration, or the day my brother William moved to Ontario. Three, it was a weeknight, and on weeknights, it's enough to get Clarissa out

of her law office and into her own home, much [...]
to someone else's. And four, she doesn't drink[...]
thought.

"Well, look what the cat dragged in," she call[...]
as I kicked off my shoes and walked through the [...]
room.

"Pardon me?" I said. This was not a typical gre[...]
in our house. We are a family that says hello to each o[...]
when one of us walks in the door. Sometimes Dad sa[...]
"Honey, I'm home," as a joke, since he's usually talk[...]
to me. Mom is never home before six-thirty. She runs h[...]
own clothing store in town, and she always makes su[...]
everything is in tip-top shape before she leaves.

"Get over here, little brother," said Clarissa, sounding as if she was sitting on a barstool somewhere,
listening to a sad old country song on the jukebox, and
another regular had just pushed in through the doors.
"Let's have a hug."

I stopped in the doorway of the kitchen and took a
good look at her. Clarissa has short, bobbed brown hair
and very funky, dark-framed glasses. She weighs eleven
pounds, soaking wet, including her clothes and jewelry.
Even Mom thinks Clarissa is too skinny, and Mom
doesn't exactly jiggle when she walks either.

"Come on," she said again, pushing her chair back
from the table. She was still wearing her work clothes,
as she called them, meaning she was dressed in a very
expensive outfit that would probably be hustled to the
cleaners before returning to hang in her closet. "What,
are you scared of your big sister all of a sudden?"

She was wobbly on her feet as she stood up.

I stepped into the kitchen and with a fine display of reluctance, because we are not a very huggy family either, I gave her a hug.

"Ahhhh," she said, slapping me on the back and holding me tight. It was a hug like you see on Oprah all the time when two people who've been fighting for fifty years suddenly decide to become friends again, although I doubt if any of those people are ever as loaded as Clarissa was, which tainted the sincerity of it all a bit. "This feels good," she said, her head squishing into my face. "This feels soooo good."

After about a minute, we broke apart. She immediately flopped into her chair. "Now go get yourself a glass from above the sink there and we'll have ourselves a drink."

"No, thanks," I said, moving towards the fridge.

"How come?"

"I had a few beers on my way home from work."

"You did?" she said, looking impressed.

"No."

"Well, come on, then. Catch up. You're a big reporter-boy now. You'll be going into the bar pretty soon. Ordering your pickled eggs and beer and watching the pretty girls play pool in their tight little jeans."

I rolled my eyes and pulled a Coke out of the refrigerator and took it over to the table.

"You ever seen a woman with a tattoo on her arm before?" said Clarissa, as she watched me sit down. I don't know how much vodka was in the bottle before she got to it, but it was only about half full now.

"Have I ever seen a what?" I said, taking a sip of my coke.

"A woman with a tattoo."

I thought for a moment. "Just Grandma. But I think hers was on her shoulder."

Clarissa gave me a look. "Just Grandma. As if. Now, I'm talking real-life here. Not in the movies. A real woman with a real tattoo on her real arm. Have you ever seen one of those before?"

"No, I haven't," I said.

"Well, those are the kind of girls I'm talking about. They're very pretty, but you have to be careful with them. Those girls always have a man nearby. If they don't come in with one, they always leave with one. I know these things. I know the kind of places you people hang out in. You don't go to the piano bars. You go to places like The Den right here in town. With the peanut shells all over the floor and the football games on. I've been in those places before. I've conducted legal discussions there."

"So, where's your family tonight, Clarissa?" I said, in an attempt to change the subject.

"My who?" she said, abruptly ending her lecture.

"Your family. Your husband and kids. Where are they tonight?"

Clarissa picked up her glass and took a deep drink. Then she put it back down on the table and looked at me. "Do you smoke, Harper?" she said.

I stared at her for a second. "Do I what?"

"Do you smoke? Cigarettes. Or cigars, too, I suppose. Those cute little Colt-thingys."

"No, I don't," I said. "Why do you ask?"

She shrugged her shoulders. "Just curious."

"Do you smoke?" I said. I was pretty sure she didn't,

but I had never thought she was the type to sit in a big empty house drinking vodka by herself either.

"No," she said. "Do you?"

"You just asked me that."

"Did I?"

"Yes."

"I'm sorry."

"It's okay."

"What did you say?"

"I said no."

"No what?"

"No, I don't smoke."

"Are you sure?"

"Of course I'm sure.

"I always thought you did."

"Well, I don't."

She took another sip of her drink. "Have you ever smoked?"

"No."

She thought for a moment. "Have you ever caused any smoke?"

This was her idea of a joke. She was referring to that fire I started in a garbage can at my school.

"Are you finished?" I said.

She giggled and picked up her glass and looked at the vodka in it. "Doesn't look like it."

"I mean with the smoke jokes."

Clarissa's eyes brightened. "That's a rhyme! Smoke jokes! What a clever boy."

I gave her a smile. "Thank you."

"You know, Mom always says you're the clever one

but I never see it. I guess I don't get out enough. Or maybe you don't get out enough, to show me."

"Maybe it's both," I said.

"See, I always thought I was the cleverest, but Mom always said, 'No, no. Harper is cleverer than you.' She never said cleverer, of course. She put it in a different way. A more intelligent way. The way Mom is."

"So where's your family?" I said again. I knew she was hiding something. Why else would she be here, getting bombed in a house that she could not wait to get out of when she was a teenager going off to university?

"You asked me that already," she said, turning serious.

"I know."

"And I told you."

"No, you didn't."

"Yes, I did."

"No, you didn't."

"Yes, I did."

I stopped before saying it again. "Okay. You told me."

"See? I told you." She giggled. "See, that's what I'm talking about. That's clever. I don't know if it's more clever than what you said, but it's clever, don't you think? I think it is. I can think of four other people at least who never would have thought of saying that."

I ignored her. "What did you tell me?"

"About what?"

"About where your family is."

"I told you where they were."

"No, you didn't."

"Yes, I did."

"No, you didn't."

"Yes, I did."

I stopped again.

"Okay. Fine. You told me where they were. Now, what are they doing there?"

Clarissa gave her shoulders an exaggerated shrug.

"Why aren't they here with you?"

She shook her head. "I don't know."

"Then why aren't you there with them?"

She did the same thing. "I'm not sure of that one either. But they've been doing it a lot lately, and I don't like it."

"Doing what?"

"Taking off without telling me where they're going."

"Why don't you follow them?"

She looked at me. Her eyes were glazed over, and they were taking on a dreamy look, as if they would be closing sometime soon. "That's a damn good idea, Harper. I should do that."

"Yes, you should," I said, although I wasn't completely sure what I was talking about.

"I think I will."

"You do that."

"Not tonight, though. Maybe tomorrow, after a good night's sleep."

"That's a good idea."

"You think so?"

"Yes, I do. I think it's a very good idea."

She smiled at me. "Well, thank you, Harper. You're a sweetheart."

"You're welcome, Clarissa." I was ready to go to bed.

"But tell me something. Tell me one more thing."

"Okay," I said.

"No. Two more things."

"Alright."

"Number two first. Are you ready?"

"I can't wait."

"Alright. Number two. Why would a grown man, in the prime of his life, all of a sudden start ignoring his beautiful wife?" She took another sip of her drink. "Why would he do that? I don't understand."

"I don't know either," I said. "Why do you ask?" As if I couldn't figure it out. In her drunken state, Clarissa had told me her reason for being at Mom and Dad's with a pile of booze in her non-existent belly and about two minutes of consciousness left in her mind.

"Because that is what my dearly beloved Michael is doing to me."

"Michael?" I said. Even though I knew she was going to say his name, I couldn't believe it when I heard it. Michael was the most devoted husband anyone in my family had ever seen, including Dad and my brother William, who are both husbands, and Mom and my sister-in-law, Jennifer, who are married to them. Michael cooked. He cleaned. He and Clarissa always did everything together, along with Byron and Amanda, of course, when they weren't dumped off at a babysitter's for a Saturday afternoon or a Sunday night, or at school all day, or away at a summer camp for two weeks, or at home with their nanny for the remaining hours between school and bedtime, which is the way it's been for them since Clarissa went back to work.

"Don't ask me why," said Clarissa, going on. "I just

said I don't know."

"I find that very hard to believe," I said. Michael did not strike me as the type to ignore his wife, whether she was beautiful or not.

"Well, it's true."

"Are you sure?"

"Of course I'm sure."

"How do you know?"

She looked at me with renewed intensity in her eyes. "I can feel it in my guts. It hits me as soon as I walk in the house. It's like walking into a place you're not wanted." She stopped talking and stared at the table. "That's only when they're all home, of course. When they've gone off somewhere, I just feel like the extra wheel. The odd man out. But I'm going to take care of that because I'm going to follow them the next time they leave the house. The next time they try to give me the slip, I'm gonna be on their tail."

I thought about that for a second. "How do you know they're slipping out of the house if you're never home?"

Clarissa didn't speak for a moment after I said that. She picked up her glass and took a small sip. I could tell, through the drunken fog that her mind was in, that she was thinking about what I had just said.

My sister's work habits were legendary, beginning with when she used to stay up for two days straight studying for an exam. Her goal was always to get every single question right, and you know, there were a few times when she did just that, even at university.

She was no different after she got married. She'd be up with the kids all day, then she'd stay up half the night reading law journals. She promised that when she went back to work after Amanda and Byron were in school, she would take it easy. That lasted for about two days.

"Well, that's the thing," she said, her eyes fixed on her glass. "They don't have to go anywhere, but they do."

"How do you know?"

"How do I know?" She lifted her head and looked at me. "I'll tell you how I know. The other day, I took the kids to a new restaurant. Never been there in their lives. This little sandwich joint down the street. I walked in the front door with them, and I was all excited to show them the fancy desserts and this big jar of dill pickles they have on the counter. But you know what the young lad says behind the counter? He says, 'Well, hello there, sweetie pies. What'll it be today? The usual?' I looked down at them and said, 'Have you been here before?' and Byron said, 'Yes. Daddy brings us here all the time.' Well, I just burst into tears right there on the spot. It was like my own two children had a secret life I knew nothing about."

She blew her nose, then she continued to talk.

"Then this afternoon I saw Michael having lunch with another woman. A big, heavyset, big-mouthed thing. She had half a cow on her plate. I swear. I swear she ordered the half-a-cow special, with fries and a small tossed salad on the side. Beverage included. I couldn't even guess at the price. I was walking by the restaurant downtown and I saw them, sitting by the window, having a little chat."

"It was probably a client," I said. Michael is a lawyer too, but for some reason he doesn't have to work as hard at it as Clarissa.

"Oh, I know. I know. I kept telling myself that. But I could not get the picture out of my head of Michael and that woman and my little angels going out and having fun together. And that's when it hit me."

"What hit you?"

She looked at me again. Her eyes were tired and sad. "I'm getting old. My life is passing me by, and I'm not getting done some of the things I've always wanted to do."

"Like what?"

"Like having another child, wearing dirty clothes in public, eating half a cow at a restaurant with my husband in the middle of a busy day."

"I've never heard you say you wanted to eat half a cow."

She shrugged. "It's an open list. I can add and subtract things as I please."

"Where does getting drunk at Mom and Dad's fit in?"

She smiled. "That's what I'm talking about. I just made this one up, spur-of-the-moment." She tried to snap her fingers, but they just rubbed softly together.

"Well, then, that's one thing on your list you've done."

She nodded. "So it is."

"So, what do you plan on doing about the others?" I was feeling genuine concern for her. Clarissa was not one to ask for help unless she desperately needed it, which is, I'm assuming, what she was doing at Mom and Dad's.

She suddenly sat up straight in her chair and touched up her hair with her fingers.

"I'm going to ask you that other question I wanted to ask you."

"You mean number one?"

"Precisely."

I repositioned myself in my chair and drained the rest of my Coke. "Alright. What is it?"

She finished with her hair and looked at me with a temporary bit of energy. "I want to know something."

"Shoot."

"I want to know if you find me attractive."

"Pardon me?"

"I want to know if you find me attractive. If Michael's going to play the field for other fish in the sea, then so am I."

I shook my head. "What makes you think Michael's out there, playing with other fish in the sea?"

"I told you about his lunchtime companion."

"I thought it was a client."

"Maybe it was."

"Well, what's wrong with taking a client out to lunch?"

"And maybe it wasn't. Now come on. This is me, at my best. A little smudgy perhaps. It's been a long day. But still, you know who you're looking at. So tell me. If you and your reporter friends were standing outside having a little chat, or sitting at a cafe somewhere, having a few beer, and you saw me walking towards you, would you take a second look, or would you just go on with your meeting?"

I closed my eyes and tilted my head towards the ceiling. I was very tired all of a sudden, and I really did not feel like doing this.

"Come on. Yes or no. Or are you visualizing right now? Is that what you're doing? Are you watching me walk down the sidewalk in your mind?"

I shook my head.

"I'm sorry. I'm interrupting. I shouldn't be doing that."

"I'm not visualizing," I said.

"Sure you are."

"No, I'm not."

"Sure you are. And there's nothing wrong with it. I'm just a person walking down the street."

"I'm not visualizing."

"Picture me in my new navy skirt, the one that goes just above the knee, and my dark boots — "

"I'm not doing that," I said. "I know what you look like. You're sitting right here. I don't have to visualize. I'm tired. I wanna go to sleep."

"I'd rather you did, now that I think about it," said Clarissa.

"Forget it," I said. "Just forget it. Do I think you're attractive? Yes. I think you're attractive. I think you look like Mom, and everybody always says that I look like Mom, too, so I would be a fool to say that I don't think you're attractive. So, yes. I think you're attractive."

She smiled. "Thank you, Harper."

"You're welcome."

"Now can you do one more thing?"

"No."

"Can you be more specific?"

"What?"

"Can you be more specific?"

"More specific?"

"Yes."

"No. I can't."

"Oh, come on."

"No."

"Why not?"

"I don't want to."

"How come?"

"Because I've had a long day today, too."

"Oh, have you? I'm sorry."

"Yes, I have. I got chewed out by my boss. I just spent two hours with some bimbo who wants to open her own card company."

"Her own what?"

"A card company. Greeting cards? Birthday cards? She's going to take on Hallmark from her basement. And I have to write about her as if she really has a chance. And to boot, I got tricked by Dad into not writing about his run for mayor."

"You what?"

"I got tricked," I said. I told her about my meeting with Kip.

"Wow. That's a bummer," she said when I finished.

"I know that."

"I'd let him know about that."

"I plan on it."

Clarissa picked up her drink and finished it off. "You should have had one of these," she said.

I nodded. "You're probably right."

"Look what it did for me. I'm feeling fine now."

"Maybe next time," I said.

She smiled again. I could see she was still very drunk, but she wasn't as close to passing out as she had been a few minutes ago. "I look forward to that," she said. Then she stood up and nearly fell on the floor, so I helped her to the spare bedroom down the hall and she collapsed on the bed as if her spine was in two pieces. I told her to go to sleep and that I would tell Mom and Dad she had the flu. Then she asked me to call Michael.

"Don't tell him I've been drinking," she called out as I was leaving the room. "I promised him I was going to stop."

I said okay and shut the door, then I phoned and left a message on their machine. Michael and the kids must have gone out again, somewhere.

< 5 >

Mom and Dad arrived home around eleven o'clock that night. They had been out campaigning at a few community events and meetings and a special dinner with the Knights of Columbus.

Mom was looking as petite and perfect as ever. She has short, (dyed) brown hair like Clarissa's. She was wearing her glasses, which she only wore when the socializing was over and it was time to settle down and relax.

Dad came in behind her. He looked tired. He was carrying more weight than he ever had in his life, and the gray in his hair was starting to take over his head. He also had his glasses on.

I came downstairs from my room to meet them at the door.

Mom asked me how my day was and I lied and said just fine. Then I told them Clarissa was sleeping in the guestroom down the hall. Dad immediately frowned and Mom turned away from hanging up her coat in the closet and said, "Why?"

There was concern in her voice, but already a touch of anger, as if she knew what I was going to say.

"Actually, she's passed out in the room down the hall," I said.

Dad closed his eyes briefly and shook his head. Mom looked hard at me.

"Tell us what's going on, Harper," she said.

I told her what I knew, which was basically everything that Clarissa had told me about the state of her relationship with Michael, plus a few observations of my own, like she seemed to be pretty drunk even before I got here, and she also seemed to know more about bars than I had suspected.

Mom finished hanging up her coat.

"Your sister knows a lot more about bars than any of us," she said, stepping into the living room.

I turned and followed her. "Meaning what?" I said.

Mom took out her earrings. "Your sister has a drinking problem, Harper. She's had one for years."

"She what?"

"It started when she was at university. Then she stopped for awhile. But it came back again after the kids were born. She drinks alone, and she gets so bombed she can't even see straight."

I was so shocked I could barely open my mouth.

"But she's very careful about it. She's still very much our little Clarissa when she's doing it. She's very organized. She goes into a nice hotel and books a room. Then she goes downstairs to the bar and gets drunk. Then she goes upstairs and sleeps it off. She never gets behind the wheel of a car. She's never drunk in her own house. She gets a wake-up call in the morning, opens the suitcase she carries in the trunk of her car, changes into a spare pair of clothes, and goes off to work looking like a million dollars. The only way Michael knows about it is when the Visa bills come in. But Clarissa pays for them all and away they go."

I was stunned.

"It's all very sad," said Mom. "We're worried sick about her but at the same time, what can we do? She's been in therapy. Michael has told her several times to just stay home with the kids. He knows how stressful she makes things for herself."

I could hear Dad hanging his coat up behind me. Then he came into the living room and loosened his tie. He flopped down in the big easy chair we have by the front window and ran his hand through his hair. Then he looked at me and gave me a sad smile.

"You're old enough to start hearing about these things," he said. "You're a big boy now."

"You mean there's more?" I said. I could feel a new emotion starting to creep in through the shock and surprise. Part of it was dread, in case there was something more, and part of it was anger.

"No," said Dad, shaking his head. "No, there's no more. But this is something you should know about now. It's time you learned more about your family and where you come from."

"Well, who said I didn't want to know about it before?" I said. The anger was starting to take over. What kind of a joke was this? I'm almost seventeen years old, and I'm hearing for the first time that my sister is an alcoholic? And the reason I'm hearing it for the first time is because Mom and Dad finally think I'm ready to handle it? How was that supposed to make me feel?

"We didn't hold anything from you," said Mom.

"Of course you did."

"No, we didn't."

"Well, what the hell else would you call it?"

"Don't swear in here, Harper," said Mom, raising her finger, as if to suggest that yes, we might be experiencing a bit of a meltdown here, but that didn't mean that Household Rule #1 could be broken, which was No Swearing, unless your name was Dad and you were trying to find Mom's wedding ring that fell down the sink in the bathroom.

"Alright," I said, cooling it for a second. "What else would you call it then? My sister has a drinking problem. Everybody in the family knows about it, even though she's very secretive, and I find out because she gets tanked right here at the house. Right in front of me."

"Not everyone in the family knows about it," said Mom.

"Who doesn't know about it?" I said.

"Well, your Auntie Rita for one."

"Auntie Rita?" I said.

"Yes."

"Who the hell cares about Auntie Rita?"

"Harper," said Dad, his voice low, meaning trouble.

"Well, who cares about Auntie Rita? She doesn't live here. She doesn't even live in this province. If she did know, I'd be going through the roof."

Mom gave me a funny look. "Why would you go

through the roof if Auntie Rita knew?"

"Because why on earth would you tell a person who still writes 'Say hi to the little ones' on her Christmas cards about Clarissa before you tell me? I'm her brother." I was practically yelling instead of talking.

Mom rolled her eyes. "Oh, come on Harper. Get off your horse. You know you and Clarissa have never been close."

"Well, no wonder. With a family like this."

"What is that supposed to mean?" said Mom.

"I mean families that keep secrets like this from each other are not exactly bonded with crazy glue, now are they."

"What?" said Mom.

"I know I've never been close to her because I've never known her, and maybe one of the reasons I've never known her is because you've kept things like this from me."

Mom sat back in her chair and tilted her head towards the ceiling. She closed her eyes and let out a deep breath.

From the other side of the room, Dad cleared his throat, but it was not in preparation for another one of his long-winded speeches about conduct in the family or cooperation or any of his other favorite themes. I think he was just clearing his throat.

"Well, all I know for sure is this is another reason to make sure she is not at the candidates' forum," said Mom, looking across the room at Dad. "That would not look good if she showed up drunk."

"What?" I said.

Mom looked at me. "What part didn't you hear?"

"Your daughter has a drinking problem and you're concerned with Dad's candidates' forum?" I said. I couldn't believe what I was hearing.

Mom looked me straight in the eye. "My daughter has had a drinking problem for the better part of the last twelve years. We have done everything we could to help her. We have also had our hands full with your brother, in case you've forgotten, and with you and your assorted escapades and brushes with the law. This is not a new crisis in our lives, Harper. We've been living with it for years. But we are not going to give her the chance to embarrass your father."

I hesitated before saying anything. She was right, to a point. This whole thing was new to me, not to them. "What makes you think she'd embarrass Dad?" I said.

"Nothing," said Mom. "But she came over here for a reason. And if she's looking for more attention, that's a great way of getting it."

"You think she came over here for attention?" I said.

"I don't know," said Mom. "But she's not going to find out about that candidates' forum."

I looked at Dad, who looked back at me and then looked away. He was not as tough as Mom when it came to things like this, but at the same time, I think he agreed with what she was saying.

"So is that something else you don't want me to put in the paper then?" I said. It was the opening I had not been looking for until the moment I said it, but as soon as the words left my mouth, I knew they'd hit the target.

"I beg your pardon?" said Mom.

I kept my eyes on Dad. "Is that something else you don't want me to put in the paper? Like when you told me not to tell anyone that you were running for mayor?"

He stared at me for a moment as he put together what I was saying.

"You say one word of this in that newspaper of yours, my boy," said Mom, who looked like she was on the verge of exploding, or at least of swearing, which would have called for an immediate rewrite of the rule book.

"I'm not saying I'm going to," I said, very calmly. "Just don't tell me what I can and can't print anymore. I don't like it, and neither does my boss."

I gave them both one final look, and then I turned and went up to my room, where I lay down in bed with my eyes wide open and stared at the ceiling.

I wasn't thinking of my little triumph in the living room, if it even was one. I was thinking about Clarissa, and what it must be like to be her right now.

I don't know what time I finally fell asleep, but I was very tired when the alarm went off in the morning.

< 6 >

On Friday, Kip called me back into his office and asked if I was ready to take to the mound again.

I had no clue what he was talking about.

"Pardon me?" I said, remembering my manners, as always, especially at times when I had no clue what people were talking about.

He made like he was a pitcher and pretended to throw a pitch in my direction. He did the wind-up and the follow-through and the whole deal, and when he was done he stood straight up and said, very seriously, as if he had just accomplished something extremely important, "Strike three." Then he made a sharp motion with his thumb. "You're outta there."

I stood in silence and wondered briefly if I had just been fired, or if I was supposed to pitch something back to him, or cheer, or what.

Finally, after blowing a bubble with his gum that would have covered his face if it had popped, he said, by way of an explanation, I think, "I'm asking if you're ready to come on in relief."

I thought about that for a moment. "Come on in what?" I said, feeling slightly stupid, since this was supposed to be the explanation.

"It's baseball talk. I need a relief pitcher. It's the top of the eighth and my arm is getting sore. I need a closer."

I narrowed my eyes. "Are you asking me to do something tonight?"

He prepared to throw another pitch and nodded. "That's exactly what I'm asking."

"What is it?" I said, feeling better.

"They're having a meet-the-candidates party at the town office today from four to six. It'll give you a chance to take a few pictures and mingle with some of the people you might be writing about over the next few weeks."

He threw another pitch.

He was obviously in a better mood than he had been over the past couple of days, which instantly put me in a better mood.

"Sure," I said, with a shrug. "I can do that."

"Get some film for the camera," he said. "And grab an extra notebook if you need it. Write down anything you hear that sounds interesting. The guy from *The Recorder* will be there, so be on your toes."

The Recorder was the other newspaper in Emville. It was run by a woman named Simone Johnson, who had a reputation for stirring the pot and causing trouble. She was someone who had no problem pointing fingers at people, and she never apologized if she pointed them at the wrong person. Dad has talked about her and some of the reporters she's hired many times over the years, and never very positively. Mom cannot stand her.

"Who is he?" I said. I could feel my stomach starting to turn. The way Kip had said it, you'd have thought I was stepping into a ring with boxing gloves on, not Town Hall for a party.

"I don't know," said Kip. "He's a high school student, just like you, so you probably know him. But I don't know what his name is." Then he said something that made me forget about my stomach and feel as good as I have in a long, long time. "I read your column by the way. I liked it."

I glowed from the inside out. "You did?" I said, without even trying to conceal my smile.

"Dixie liked it, too," he added. "So did Paula, but she likes anything."

It was my first one. I had written about the whole process of getting a job at the paper and what it felt like to sit down at a desk that was not in my bedroom and write words and stories that would actually be read by people who were not relatives or classmates or schoolteachers.

I started off by detailing my previous experience as a reporter. It went like this.

My career as a writer began at our school newspaper. It is called Ragtime, *and for awhile I contributed to its pages by writing fascinating stories about why the cafeteria serves french fries with every meal (because they go with everything) and which teachers drive the nicest cars (Mr. Thompson and his Porsche, until Toby Ryerson smoked it with his Camaro, and Ms. Wallace, who could drive in anything and make it look good). Then I had the bright idea to write a column, so I did. I wrote a column called Fly On The Wall for almost six whole months and managed to conceal my identity almost entirely until this very minute.*

But now, as a bigshot work-experience reporter with Emville's official number one newspaper, I have my sights set on bigger game, like politics, current affairs, and even (yikes!) sports.

I am excited, but also scared. At school, only the teachers see your work. They usually have a red pen in their hand when they're reading it, which is unfortunate, but at least they keep your marks a secret from everyone else, and never in the history of education has a student ever been fired for writing poorly. Failed, yes; but never fired.

Out here in the jungle, it's a different situation. It's arranging facts and gathering quotes and meeting deadlines. It's doing rewrites and snapping pictures.

I carry a notepad, two pens, and a pencil wherever I go. The second pen is in case the first one runs out of ink, and the pencil is in case both pens run out, or if I have to write against a wall, or on a surface where a pen might not work.

I have spare change in my pocket in case I have to make a phone call. I read news magazines for story ideas and have now completely memorized what MLA and MP stand for, and what the difference between the two is.

I have (sort of) figured out right-wing politics

*from left-wing, and municipal government from
provincial and federal.*

*I listen to talk shows on the radio when I'm
bored, but still.*

*I do not know where this gig as a reporter will
take me. I may pursue a career in journalism. I
may not. But as for now, I want to enjoy the experience as much as I can.*

I hope that means you will, too.

"Well, that's good," I said to Kip, in the understate-
ment of the year. "I'm glad to hear that."

I wasn't kidding, either. I had left out all the parts
about Kip bawling me out and feeling like a fool for
missing that story about Dad, and I was hoping he
wouldn't say anything about it.

"So am I," said Kip, who had apparently finished
pitching. "I don't have time to write another column.
Now, let's get moving."

I left for Town Hall fifteen minutes later. I was still
buzzing over the reaction to my column, and also about
getting a real assignment again. For the past few days,
all Kip had given me to write were business features,
which are very boring and have nothing to do with the
news or being a reporter. Tom always says that without
them there would be less advertising, and with less advertising there would be less newspaper, meaning, I
think, no more me.

I'm sure this is very true, but I still think they're boring.
You sit there and listen to some person tell you how great
their little store is, or how big and booming their busi-

ness is going to become, and then you have to write about it, except you can't check their facts to see if they're actually telling the truth or not, and you can't throw in an opinion anywhere. You just write what they tell you to write, only you put it even better, so it sounds as good as it possibly can, which sometimes can be quite a stretch.

But I was done with those for the moment and I was feeling more like a real reporter than ever before as I turned the corner and cut across the parking lot that would take me to Town Hall. Then I saw Rufus Monahan leaning against the wall next to the front doors. He was smoking a cigarette, as usual, and looking like a worm.

Rufus Monahan goes to the same school as I do. He's in the same grade. He calls himself a writer. Technically, when you think about it, we should be friends. But we aren't. Rufus doesn't have any friends. He's too much of a weasel. He even looks like a weasel with his long, pointy nose and darting eyes. He's short and skinny and he smokes a pack a day, which is something, considering that for about seven hours a day from Monday to Friday he's in a classroom.

He worked for the school paper last year, until he was fired for constantly getting into fights with the editor and the other reporters and the people he was supposed to be writing about and Mr. Gomez, the teacher who was assigned to watch over the newspaper staff.

"You're creating too much dissension," said Mr. Gomez, who leaned a bit on the soft side when it came to getting mad.

"Is that supposed to bother me?" said Rufus, sticking

a smoke in his mouth.

"Well, apparently, it doesn't," said Mr. Gomez. "And that's the trouble. That's why I'm asking you to leave."

"Aw, you're making me cry," said Rufus, lighting a match, even though he was still on school property. "I need a hug before I break down."

He nodded his head as I walked towards him. "Hey, Peanuts," he said. Rufus called everyone he knew Peanuts, even people who were in grade twelve.

"What are you doing here, Rufus?" I said. I wasn't thinking clearly, or else I would have figured it out myself.

"I'm here to run your old man outta town," he said, with a sneer. Then he laughed. He had a sick, snivelly laugh, like a villain in one of those old, cheesy, horror movies. "What do you think I'm here for? I'm here for the same thing you are. To meet all these lousy pugs who think they're gonna turn our town into New York City."

"What?" I said. I was so turned off by his laugh that I didn't even understand what he was talking about.

"I'm here as a reporter, Peanuts. Just like you are. I'm the new hound dog at *The Recorder*. I'm here to sniff around until I find out what's going on. And if I don't, I get swatted by old lady Johnson." He dropped his smoke and mashed it with his foot. Then he went on. "This is it for me, Peanuts. I break a coupla stories here and its bye-bye Phlegmville and hello to the big town. This is the job I've been waiting for."

Now I knew what he was talking about.

"You're the competition?" I said. I was nervous again. Rufus was the most unlikable person on the planet, and that was exactly what made him the best reporter our school newspaper has ever had. Even Mr. Gomez admitted it, after he gave Rufus the heave-ho. "That boy would ask any person any question to get to the bottom of a story," he said, shaking his head. "It's a shame he doesn't know when to turn it off."

To boot, his uncle was a bigshot at a paper out east. Rufus used to yap endlessly about all the rich people his Uncle Eugene had "brought down." That was the term he always used — brought down.

"The competition?" said Rufus, looking amused. "Heh, heh. That's a good one, Peanuts. That's a funny one."

"What's so funny about it?" I said, trying to untangle my backbone so I could stand up to him.

Rufus took a step towards me. I could smell his stinking smoke-breath on my face. "We're in a different league, Peanuts. I might be competition for you, but you're nothing to me. My old lady's cat coughs bigger hair balls than the problems you'd give me on an election trail."

"How big's her cat?" I said. I didn't want to get pushed around by him before things even got started.

He kept his eyes on me. "It's a little pussycat named Fudgee-O. All brown and soft in the middle. Cute little cuddly thing, just like you."

I took a small step towards him. Between the two of us, Rufus and I couldn't fight off a cold with a crate of Dristan and a tub of homemade chicken soup, but I wanted to show him that I was not about to step back and let him get all the good stories.

"You'll see how cuddly I am a month from now," I said. It was a very weak threat, I know, but it was also the first one I've ever said to anyone outside my family, and I didn't exactly have much time to come up with something clever.

Rufus lifted a squished pack of cigarettes from his shirt pocket and tapped out another smoke. He put it in his mouth and took out his matches and handed them to me.

"What's this?" I said.

"Do me a favor, Peanuts. Light my cigarette for me," he said.

"Why?"

"Look at my hand. It's shaking."

"Knock it off," I said.

"I'm scared, Peanuts. Really. You're frightening me."

"Get outta the way, Rufus. I've got work to do."

He put the unlit cigarette back in his pocket.

"Let's go in together," he said, sounding cheery all of a sudden. "Like a team. You go to the left. I'll go to the right. We'll meet back in the middle and compare notes."

"What?" I said. He couldn't be serious.

"I'm serious," he said. "That's the way it's done. It's you versus me, but first, it's us versus them."

I thought about that for a moment. It made sense, especially after what Kip had said about Dad and all the other politicians he had followed over the years. But still, there was something about Rufus that I knew I couldn't trust.

"Look," he said, with some impatience, as if he was already tired of carrying me along. "No one's gonna be saying anything at this little tea party. Wait until they're alone, at their kitchen table where they don't think anyone else can hear them. That's when you get your claws out. The only good thing about these things is the dessert table."

I stared at him for a second, and then I nodded, and we went in.

The room we were led to was already filled with people, all of them smiling and shaking hands and enjoying themselves. Most of them had small cups of coffee or juice in their hands, or paper plates with cheese and crackers or a pastry.

I followed my orders and turned to the left. I had my camera around my neck with the flash already on, and my notepad in my hand. I introduced myself to people and took pictures of all the candidates. I tried to take candid shots, where they pretended they didn't know that I was right beside them, lining up a picture, but not everyone liked that approach, so for two or three of them I found a relatively quiet spot in the room and asked them to smile while they stared at me.

I asked all of them the same creative questions, like why were they running and what they thought their chances were.

One of them, Sam Potts, who was one of the two people running for mayor against Dad, said it didn't really matter why he was running because he didn't stand a chance of winning.

"Why not?" said a voice beside me. It was Rufus, from out of nowhere.

Potts gave Rufus a look. "Because Winslow's got it in the bag, that's why."

"You think so?" said Rufus, scribbling madly in his notebook.

I decided I should probably do the same.

"Of course," said Potts. He was a big, gray-haired man with a pot-belly that practically stuck outside the door. "He's from the same club as all the other old boys. They're not gonna let anybody new get in."

"Why not?" said Rufus, who didn't even look up from his pad when he asked the question.

"I'd spoil all the fun. I'd break up their party."

"What party?" said Rufus, egging him on.

"All these tax cuts they've been handing out. The deals with these developers. The land in this town is disappearing faster than whisky at a fishing derby, and we can't get it back."

"You think council is caving in to big business?" said Rufus.

"I think money talks in this town, boys," said Potts, preparing to leave. "And I don't like what it's been saying."

Rufus finished writing. "Can I get your number, sir? I'd like to give you a call one day next week. Maybe we could sit down and have a little chat."

Potts rattled off his phone number. I wrote it down as fast as Rufus did.

"Thank you for your time, sir," said Rufus, with a nod, when we were done.

Sam Potts nodded back and left to mingle with the others.

"That was fast," I said, turning to Rufus. I felt like my head was actually spinning on my neck. For two minutes I hadn't said a word, and yet I had just recorded the best interview of my life as a reporter.

"That's the way you gotta work, Peanuts. You get a guy like that in here who's ready to wag his chin, you gotta be ready."

Wag his chin? I felt like saying. Where did that come from?

But before I could ask, Rufus began talking again.

"Now, where's your old man, Peanuts?" he said, looking around the room.

"My who?" I said. I was not used to people referring to Dad as an old man.

"Your dad," said Rufus, making a face. "Your father. The Big Peanut Man. Where is he?"

"I don't know," I said. "Why?"

"I wanna talk to him."

"About what?"

"Never mind," said Rufus, and he took off across the room. I followed him to the other side where I saw Dad, who must have arrived while we were talking to Potts, leaning against the wall talking with someone. Rufus cut into the conversation like he was passing on an important message and began asking Dad questions.

"Dr. Winslow, one of the other candidates for mayor has accused the current council of running an old boys' club that caters to the demands of big business. What do you have to say about that?"

Dad looked at Rufus before answering, and then over at me. At first he seemed annoyed at the intrusion, and possibly a bit confused, since this was the first time he and I had crossed paths like this. But he settled down quickly. He had been a politician for more years than I have been alive and, as Mom has pointed out many times, he is very good at it.

"The current council has done a very effective job attracting new businesses and land developments to our town. We've also said no to some of them. We've also built three new playgrounds, further developed the pathways around Ferguson Lake, created a brand new park for skateboarders, and we've hired an architect for plans for the new arena. So I don't think we cater to big business at all, other than to say that we listen to anyone who's interested in coming to our town, and if there's something we can do to help, we'll look at it."

"So you'll bend the rules to let the right people in?" said Rufus.

Dad smiled. "Everything we do is in accordance with our rules. We do not bend them. We follow them."

"What about cutting taxes in the industrial park?"

"What about it?" said Dad.

"Isn't that bending the rules?"

"No."

"Isn't it changing the rules?"

"Not if everyone agrees with it."

"Who's everyone? The old boys' club?"

Dad gave Rufus a look. "I don't think Lois McGovern or Ruth Shultz or Pat Lewis would appreciate you calling them old boys. And I don't think whoever you were talking to really knows what is going on at the town office. Now if you'll excuse me." He nudged past Rufus and came to a stop at me. "You getting all this down?" he said.

I nodded.

"Good boy. I'll see you at home."

He slipped past me and into the crowd. Rufus finished writing in his notepad, then turned to me and made a motion towards the door. We went outside, where he reached into his pocket for a smoke and started to nod his head.

"That's a good little story we got in there, Peanuts. That'll keep everyone happy. Some guy takes on your dad. Your dad counters back. That'll look okay in the papers."

I stood and said nothing.

"You see the way it works? Attack, defend. Counter-attack. Counter-defend. That's the way it goes. Especially in elections. You get some of these guys saying, 'Oh, I just want to help the town grow,' and I stand there thinking to myself, 'You bozo. You don't stand a chance with that attitude.' That's why I jumped at that pot-bellied guy. I heard him say to you that he doesn't stand a chance to win the election. Well, I hear that and I start thinking, that's a guy who's feeling cheated already. He wants into the game. He wants some attention. And at this point of it all, he'll get it. Nothing else is happening. Might as well give the headlines to the little people."

He pulled on his smoke.

"How come you know so much about this?" I said. So what if he had an uncle in the newspaper business? I have an uncle who owns a car dealership, but you don't see me wearing a plaid jacket with money spilling out of the pockets, do you? No, you certainly don't.

"I study it," said Rufus. "I read the papers like these university eggheads read Shakespeare. I go to press conferences to hear the questions they ask. I go to scrums to see how they corner a guy and make him talk. And then I read the papers the next day to see how they turn a simple little comment into headline news."

He finished his smoke. "You should do the same, Peanuts. You were pretty quiet in there. I could have gone off quietly into the night, phoned these people up, and scooped you like a clump of dirt in a steam shovel. But I didn't. Next time I might though."

I was tempted to thank him, but I kept my mouth shut. I knew that wouldn't look good.

Then we parted company and I went back to the office, where I wrote the story about Sam Potts and Dad and left it on Kip's desk.

On the one hand, I felt good because I knew it was a strong piece. But on the other hand, I felt a bit guilty, knowing that Rufus probably could have left me in the dark back there at the party, and I wouldn't have even known it until Tuesday morning, when the next edition of the paper came out.

< 7 >

Kip invited me into his office for a drink Tuesday night.
Dixie and Tom came in as well, but Kip told me that the
occasion was specifically for me, in recognition of my
"fine work on the weekend," meaning Friday night.

Tom brought in a couple of extra chairs and Dixie
plunked an ashtray on Kip's desk, even though smoking
in the office was generally not allowed.

"It's after work hours," said Dixie, lighting a cigarette, as if she truly believed that the time of day made a
difference.

"So what?" said Tom. "We're all still in the building."

"Doesn't matter," said Dixie, and she sat back in her
chair and got herself comfortable as Kip pulled a bottle
of whisky out of his drawer, and a stack of plastic cups.
Then he started pouring.

"Harper?" said Dixie, passing me a glass. "What do
you usually take with your whisky?"

"What do I usually take with my whisky?" I said.

"Yes."

"I don't usually take anything with my whisky."

Dixie raised her eyebrows and gave me a little nod. She was impressed. "Good for you. You drink it straight. Like a man should."

"I don't usually drink whisky is what I'm saying."

"Oh," she said, unfazed. "What is your drink then?"

I thought for a moment. In my life, I have had maybe three cups of coffee, no tea, two beers, and not a single drop of hard liquor. "I don't really have a drink," I said, holding the glass of whisky in my hand. It could have been a urine sample for all the interest I had in it.

"Ladies and gentlemen," said Kip, putting the bottle down and picking up his glass. "It gives me great pleasure to officially welcome our very own Harper Winslow to our award-winning news department. Congratulations, Harper. You did a helluva job."

He was talking about the story I had written.

I had started it like this:

Mayoralty candidate Sam Potts conceded Friday night that the contest for mayor was virtually over already.

"Winslow's got it in the bag," said Potts, referring to fellow candidate Dr. Benjamin Winslow. "He's from the same club as all the other old boys. They're not gonna let anybody new get in."

Potts, a newcomer to Emville's political scene, was speaking at a Meet-the-Candidates forum last week at Town Hall. The third candidate running for mayor, George Morrison, was out of town and did not attend the function.

But Potts, citing a recent run of large new businesses and grand housing developments, declared that the current council was being swayed too much by money and not enough by the best interests of the people.

"All these tax cuts they've been handing out. The deals with these developers. The land in this town is disappearing faster than whisky at a fishing derby, and we can't get it back."

For his part, Winslow maintained that the town has struck a fine balance between accepting and rejecting applications for new businesses and housing projects, as well as in taking care of the facilities Emville already has.

"The current council has done a very effective job attracting new businesses and land developments to our town. We've also said no to some of them. We've also built three new playgrounds, further developed the pathways around Ferguson Lake, created a brand new park for skateboarders, and we've hired an architect for plans for the new arena."

Kip even ran it on the front page, beneath the headline, "Candidate calls run for mayor over: Claims 'old boys'' club too tough to beat."

"To Harper," said Dixie, who, I had come to realize, loved these special events.

"To Harper," said Tom, who had a can of V8 juice in one hand, and a Styrofoam bowl of cooked green beans in the other.

"Tell me you're not bringing green beans to a party,"

Dixie had said when Tom had first walked into Kip's office.

"I need the carbs," Tom had said.

"To me," I said, completing the toast. I touched glasses all around, including Tom's can, but I did not take a sip of my drink until Dixie said, "Come on, Harper. Sip it, like it's hot chocolate. But please don't blow on it first. I had a boyfriend who did that once. He was such an idiot."

"I don't know," I said, staring into my cup. I did not see pleasure or enjoyment there. Just an inch or two of liquid that made my eyes water when I tried to sniff it.

"Oh, come on," said Dixie again. "We're here for you. You have to drink."

"Give him a drum roll, Tom," said Kip. Tom put down his juice and beans and started slapping his hands on his legs like a drummer you would hear at a circus or a show of some kind that means people are waiting for something to happen.

He kept it up for about a minute and showed no signs of slowing down, so I took a sip. I held it in my mouth for a moment before I swallowed, and then I gulped it down, and my head exploded. My eyes watered. My throat burned. For a moment, I thought I had swallowed a torch.

Dixie, between snorts of laughter, handed me a glass of water.

"What's that gonna do?" said Kip, who was enjoying the show I was putting on as much as she was.

"I don't know," said Dixie. "Something. Look at the poor kid."

"Want some of these?" said Tom, handing me his

bowl of beans. "They're absorbent. I think."

I drank the water. It seemed to help, although I don't know how.

"You'll feel better in a few minutes," said Dixie, re-assuringly, like a nurse, or the mother of a small child with the flu, or pretty well anyone other than a person sitting in a grubby little office with a smoke in one hand and a glass of poison in the other. "God," she added, shaking her head and looking at me. "You're making me remember how I felt after my first drink of whisky."

"How long ago was that?" said Kip, leaning back in his chair and looking ready to start up a conversation.

"I don't know," said Dixie, pausing to reflect.

"Come on. Tell us," said Kip.

"I don't know."

Kip thought for a moment. "I bet you were about six," he said.

Dixie gave him a look. "Get out."

"I bet you were twenty," said Tom.

Dixie shook her head. "I wasn't twenty. That I know for sure."

"How about seven," said Kip.

"Go away," said Dixie.

"Seven-and-a-half, then," said Kip.

Dixie looked at him again. "I was ten at least."

"Oh, ten," said Kip. "You were a big girl."

"That's the year I met my cousin Pixie. She was a wild one, that one. She introduced me to a lot of stuff. I learned a whole bunch that year."

"Pixie?" said Tom.

"That was her name," said Dixie, taking a sip of her drink.

"Pixie and Dixie?" said Kip, looking like he might get sick.

"Her real name was Patricia, but after she met me, and we became so close, people started calling her Pixie. It was cute. We liked it."

"That's enough to make me pour this out the window," said Kip, looking at his drink.

I'm all for that, I felt like saying, but of course, I didn't.

"Pixie and Dixie and my little neighbor Eddie," said Dixie, staring at the floor. "We were the three amigos, and boy, did we stir up trouble."

"I was fourteen," said Kip, putting his drink on his desk. "At a hockey tournament in Winnipeg. The parents were all having a party in the coach's room at the hotel. Then someone pulled the fire alarm. Everybody ran downstairs except me and my buddy, Kenny Williams. We snuck inside their room, swiped a bottle of whisky, and hid it in our room."

"Well, weren't you the little brat," said Dixie, looking impressed.

"When I was fourteen, I was bench-pressing two hundred pounds and doing three paper routes at a time," said Tom. "I've never touched a drop of alcohol in my life."

Dixie looked him over. "That's because you hang out with dumbbells all the time."

"That's because I'm smart," said Tom.

"Hey, I was smart," said Kip. "First I pulled the fire alarm. Then we jammed the coach's door before it closed all the way."

"Then you got stinkin' drunk and threw up all over the bathroom in your hotel room," said Tom, finishing

Kip's story for him. "Then you got thrown off the hockey team and you've never traveled anywhere else with a group of people ever again."

Kip shook his head. "That's not what happened."

"No?"

"No."

"Tell me what happened then."

"Kenny Williams got sick in the bathroom. I puked in the hot tub upstairs. It was full of people at the time, and they all left in one smooth, very fast motion."

"Now that's using your brain," said Tom.

"The manager was not happy," said Kip. "Neither was the coach. Neither was my dad."

"Did you ever touch another drop of whisky?" said Dixie, smiling, as if she already knew what the answer was going to be.

"Soon as we got home," said Kip.

Tom turned and looked at me. "See, Harper. These are the influences you can choose from. Me, a self-made bodybuilder/fitness buff and businessman, or them, a pair of watered-down storytellers who'll be doing the same things fifty years from now. If they're alive."

"Oh, come on, Tom," said Dixie. "Harper has other influences in his life besides us. He has his lovely mother and father."

"His girlfriend," said Kip.

"You never told me you had a girlfriend," said Dixie, her eyes swinging to me.

"You never asked," I said, being clever.

"Well, now I am," said Dixie. She turned in her chair so she was directly facing me. "Tell me about her. Who is she? Why isn't she here, making sure you're okay. Making sure these big bullies don't push you around."

I gave them the lowdown on my girlfriend, Sunny. I told them how we had met at a writing camp last summer, and how much fun we had together, and all the things we did before she left for an art school in Toronto in the fall. I even told them about the last time she phoned my house to talk to me. "My mom answered, and the two of them talked about bras for the next forty minutes."

A brief moment of silence followed.

"Bras?" said Dixie.

"The liquid-lift bra, to be specific," I said, wondering why my head was feeling so light all of a sudden. I looked down at my drink and finished it off. "I guess they're quite the thing in Ontario. Sunny said every store she goes into has them."

"Really?" said Dixie.

"Apparently," I said, with a shrug. "You know, on those little mannequin things."

"Oh, yes."

I looked at Dixie. "I used to stare at those all the time when I was a kid."

"You don't say," said Dixie, an amused look on her face.

"Oh, yes." I nodded my head. It felt heavy and light at the same time. "I used to wander off in the underwear department when Mom was in the fitting room, trying something on."

"And what did you find?" said Dixie.

"All sorts of stuff," I said, trying to remember. "There

was one part of the old Eaton's store that I liked going into. Lots of those big posters on the walls, and little pictures on the underwear boxes."

"Some of those bras are pretty expensive," said Dixie.

"I never checked the price," I said. My eyelids were getting heavy. "I wasn't in there to buy anything. I was just there to kick the tires, so to speak. Look around. See what's new."

"You know," said Kip, topping up his drink. "I've had a lot of girlfriends in my day."

"Oh, boy," said Tom. "Here we go."

"Oh, please, Kip," said Dixie. "One disgusting hot tub story is enough for tonight, thank you."

"And I've talked to a lot of fathers," said Kip, ignoring their comments. "And we've talked about a lot of things. Sports. Politics. The weather. Current affairs."

"Lingerie?" said Tom.

"Quiet," said Kip, raising a finger. "I'm getting to that."

"Oh, oh," said Tom. "Get your notepad out, Harper. A new front page story's coming."

"But not once," continued Kip, "not once did I ever chat about underwear with any of them. Not once."

"Considering your track record, maybe you should have," said Dixie.

"Hey, you know what?" said Tom, putting down his empty bowl of beans. "I have talked about underwear with one of my girlfriends' fathers. Joe Heatherington. I went out with his daughter about five years ago. He used to work for this place called The Men's Store downtown. They had the best underwear you could buy there, and I used to get it all at halfprice."

"No kidding," said Dixie.

"No kidding," said Tom, shaking his head. "It was nice stuff, too. Fit well. Was always nice and comfortable. Hundred percent cotton."

"Well, thank you for sharing that," said Dixie, with a polite smile.

"I'm serious," said Tom. "This stuff I'm wearing now — it rides all over the place. I got outta my car the other day …"

"I think you've told us all we need to know," said Dixie.

"Hey," said Kip in a loud voice, pretending to check his watch. "He's only been talking about it for two minutes. Give him thirty-eight more. Forty minutes. That's how long Harper's mom, Sunny, and his girlfriend were talking."

"Oh, come on," said Dixie, rolling her eyes.

"It's not my mom, Sunny," I said, correcting Kip. "It's my girlfriend, Sunny, and my mom."

"Whatever," said Kip. "Now, go on, Tom. Tell us more about your underwear."

Tom hesitated.

"Come on," said Kip. "Does it wash well? Does it come in different colors? Different themes?"

"Different themes?" said Dixie.

"You know. Spaceships. Westerns. Cartoons. The little pictures they put on the front and back."

"Oh, I see what you mean," said Dixie, nodding her head. "I know what you're talking about."

"They've got all kinds of things on there now," said Kip.

"The cartoons are fun," said Dixie. "I've seen those before."

"Do they have themes like that for your stuff?" said Kip, turning serious for a moment, to Dixie. "You know, little Barbie things, or anything like that?"

"Little Barbie things?" said Dixie.

"You know what I mean."

She shook her head. "I'm sorry. But as far as I know, they don't."

"No?" said Kip, looking concerned.

"No, we're very boring that way," said Dixie. "None of our lingerie has cartoons."

"Well, neither do mine," Tom said to Dixie, "in case you were wondering."

Dixie made a face like she had just tasted something sour. "I wasn't," she said. "Trust me. But thanks just the same."

Tom nodded, as if to say "Not a problem," and reached into his bag for some carrots.

"What about you, Harper? What kind of artwork is on your boxer shorts this evening?" said Dixie.

"I'm not sure," I said. I closed my eyes to think. The room tilted to the right and I reached out and grabbed Tom to keep from falling off my chair. Then I opened my eyes and tried to focus, but everything was still bobbing back and forth.

"Oh, oh," I heard Dixie say. "Looks like someone's reached his limit."

"Looks like someone might need some new underwear

pretty soon," said Kip.

"I'll drive him home," said Tom, standing up. "You two winos can walk."

"Can we?" said Dixie, as a joke.

I do not remember anything more about that night, other than Tom drove me home and carried me upstairs to bed before Mom and Dad arrived.

I had a headache the whole next day, and for awhile I thought I was going to be sick, but when I got to work, Kip told me that I was going to be the new courthouse reporter, starting Thursday.

"I'm what?" I said. My headache disappeared in three seconds.

"I'm tied up with the election," he said. "You're next in line. So be there as soon as you can after school. They usually start around two, so if you think you've missed something, check the docket at the front desk. Otherwise, sit in there with your notepad open and write down anything that looks good."

I couldn't believe it.

"And remember to wear clean underwear," said Dixie, as a final joke.

I laughed, and I kept on laughing all the way home.

< 8 >

I wrote my next column that night, before my big day at court. I wanted to get everything out of the way in case something happened.

I do not usually operate at such a high level of efficiency. At school, I scramble to get my assignments in on time, or, failing that, before the penalties kick in.

My math teacher, Mr. Kendrick, who looks exactly like a math teacher, with big black-rimmed glasses and the worst clothes you could ever imagine a person wearing, treats everything we take home like an income tax return, or so he said, meaning, I think, since I've never actually filled out an income tax return, that if we're late, we get penalized every day until we hand it in. "It is time you learned about responsibility," he said on the first day of classes.

My English teacher, Ms. Marsden, has a big basket on her desk that we have to drop our writing journals in every Friday so she can go through them on the weekend. We get an automatic ten percent towards our final mark if we write something every day and hand it in to her every week. But if you miss one week, you get cut down to five percent, and if you miss two weeks, you get zero.

I have had to run the full length of the school many times to drop my journal into her stupid basket on a Friday afternoon. She always does the same thing when I do this: She peers at me from above her glasses and gives me a look that says, "Wasn't I supposed to have this an hour ago, young man?"

I never stop and talk to her. Her interests in writing go in a completely different direction than mine. I did tell her once that I was writing for the newspaper, though. She said, "How nice," and left it at that. A little encouragement would have been better, or a smile, or even a simple, "Well, good for you," but I was talking about an after-school activity, so I guess she would have been stepping above and beyond her duties to say anything more than what she did.

But really, I couldn't care less what she thinks. My future as a writer is going to be writing for newspapers and magazines and books of my own, not book reports and character sketches because some woman with a degree on her wall wants me to.

Half the time, I don't even think she wants us to do that, but what else would we do with all the time we spend together? How else would she prove to the principal that we were actually doing something? That's why I think so many teachers make their students do so much work: to make it look like we're all doing something.

The exciting thing about writing for *The Express* is, it makes me feel like my future is right now. Every night I sit at my desk in the office, or at my computer at home, and blast away at the keys. I imagine myself to be every writer I have ever seen sitting in front of a keyboard, like Elmore Leonard stretched out with his laptop on his legs, or E.B White writing *Charlotte's Web* with his sleeves rolled up at his old typewriter. I could be Hemingway, who I don't even really know that well, but who has a fine reputation, or Mickey Spillane, writing an entire mystery novel in one day.

I never think of being one of the classic writers, though, like Shakespeare. They're too old. And those quill pens and the little cups of ink they use always re-mind me of taking notes at school.

But anyway. I had a column to write and so I spent a couple of hours upstairs in my room writing it. Mom poked her head in once to ask how I was doing, and Dad came upstairs to say he saw the story I had written about him. He's been so busy lately that we hadn't even seen each other since Monday, the day before the paper came out. "You did a good job," he told me. "You handled that very well."

I thanked him, then I got back to work.

My column went like this:

> *I have never covered an election before.*
>
> *I have seen them unfold on television, sort of, since I have never been really interested in them, until now. My dad has been a source of stories and information over the years, but as for experiencing it all on a firsthand level, this is my maiden voy-age. My (hopefully not exactly)* Titanic *adventure.*
>
> *So far, it has been a fascinating one.*
>
> *I met most of the candidates last week. They seemed to be a thoughtful, respectable bunch.*

*Many of them told me that they were running
because they wanted to see better services in our
community, or safer streets, or lower taxes. One
person, Stan Wallace, told me that he wanted to be
elected so he could light the fire under council's
butt and get Emville back on the map. Tony
Peterson, who, at 22, is the youngest candidate,
said he put his name on the list of nominees because he couldn't find a job and his parents
thought being a town councilor would look good
on his resume, which it would, I assume.*

*Dolores Reeson, one of five women involved in
this election, summarized her platform this way:
"The first time some slicker from the city walks
into town with a proposal to take over some more
of our farm land, I'll stick a hot poker up his you-
know-what and drive him right outta town."*

*She said this while standing next to a Thank You
For Not Smoking sign with a cigarette in her mouth.*

*Matilda Jenkins spoke nonstop for several
minutes when I asked her why she was interested in
politics. "I do not settle for second best," she told
me, in what proved to be her usual, rapid-fire way
of talking. "And I will not let my town settle for
second best either. I am an activist. That is how I
spend my time, improving the world around me,
helping others, becoming a better person. I go to
church every Sunday, with my family, of course. I
pay my bills in person, so I can see who I'm handing
my money to. I vote with my head, not with my heart.
People who vote with their heart usually know*

they're not voting for the right person, they just can't bear the thought of voting for someone else, which I think is just plain stupid and ridiculous."

Later, on the subject of her chances on election day, she said, "I think my track record speaks for itself. I've done more for this town in the last five years than any individual councilor we have now has done in a lifetime. The people know that. They know my husband. They know our children. They know me. They know what they'll get when they vote for me. I am a very logical person. I'm a doer, not a sitter. If they want someone who sits around all day, forming committees and sub-committees, then they're better off voting for someone else. But if they want to see some actual changes in the community, then they should go with me."

In two weeks, we find out who will actually form our next council.

I think any one of the people I met would do a fine job in their own right, but remember, what do I know? I can interview these people, and write about them, and take their picture, but I'm not old enough to vote yet.

In other words, my role in the outcome of this election ends right here, at the exact same point that your role, as voters, begins.

I read it over a couple of times, and then I went to bed. I didn't pick up a book to read or anything. I just went straight to bed. I wanted to be well-rested for tomorrow.

< 9 >

I ran into Rufus on Thursday after school. He was standing outside the cafeteria, looking as squirmy as ever.

He smiled when he saw me.

"Peanuts," he said, moving away from the wall. He came right up close and started to walk with me to my locker. "What are you up to?"

I'm going to the courthouse, I could have said, but I didn't. I felt no need to tell him what I was up to.

"It's a court day, y'know," he said, before I could say anything. "You heading over there, or are you goin' somewhere else?"

I stopped at my locker. "Right now, I'm not going anywhere," I said, which was the absolute truth.

"I'm going to talk to someone," said Rufus. I guess he was afraid that I wasn't going to ask.

"Who?" I said, although I really didn't care, or so I liked to believe.

He smiled at me again. I could see his yellow teeth.

"Who do you think?"

"I don't know."

"Good. Let's keep it that way."

I opened my locker and put my books inside and grabbed my backpack. I wanted to go before I missed anything, but now I was curious about who he was going to see.

"Let me guess," I said.

"Go ahead."

"That big mouth we talked to at the party the other day. Potts."

Rufus gave me a look. "*We* talked to?" he said. "Wasn't it me who did most of the talking, and you who sponged all the good quotes and turned it into a front page story?"

I shrugged my shoulders. "Alright. The guy you talked to."

"I'm surprised you had the nerve to run your name under the headline," he said.

"I still wrote the story."

"Barely. After I fed it to you on a spoon. I gave it to you like an old lady feeding her baby. 'Here you go sweetiepie. Here you go. Whoopsie. Don't spill any now. Here, lemme help.'"

"Alright, Rufus," I said. I'd had enough of him for the day already. "I gotta go."

"Where?"

"Out."

"Out where?"

"Of here."

"To where?"

"None of your business."

"The courthouse?"

"Maybe."

"Town Hall?"

"Possibly."

"You got somebody coming in to the office?"

"Perhaps."

I was seeing now how paranoid Rufus could get over this "scoop" business.

"Tell me. We could work together. Just like the last time."

His boss must be meaner than I thought.

"I don't want to," I said.

"Come on. I'll give you a call tonight. Around ten."

"I won't be home."

"Where will you be?"

I looked at him. I was ready to leave now. My locker was closed and I had everything I needed on my back.

"I'll be out getting drunk," I said. Even the thought of it made my stomach roll. But he didn't have to know that.

"Drunk?" said Rufus.

"Yes."

"Why will you be getting drunk?"

"Why not?" I said.

"Well, are you celebrating something?"

I hesitated. I had never expected to have a conversation like this with Rufus Monahan, who always struck me as the kind of person who couldn't care less what anybody else was doing.

"It's my birthday," I told him.

"It is?"

"No," I said, brushing past him. "But I'm sure it's somebody's."

I arrived at the courthouse shortly after three, just in time for the judge to call for a break, so I scanned the docket on the front counter to see what was coming up next. There were no major crimes to report on, which was not a big surprise. There hadn't been one in Emville for years. No hostage-taking dramas. No death-defying car chases or middle-of-the-night bank robberies.

For that reason alone, crimes that were not usually considered to be big ones, like bicycle theft, *were* considered to be big ones when it came to stories in *The Express*'s Court Briefs section. And everyone in town read the Court Briefs. Everyone. Even people who didn't read the paper read the Court Briefs. That's why it was such a thrill for me to be writing them. The stories were short, they named names, and, according to Mom, they were "fun."

"Fun?" I said, after I told her and Dad what I would be doing.

"Yes," said Mom. "They're fun. I like to read them. It's real drama you're seeing over there, and when these people who commit a crime go to court, I call it fun. I'm glad they're caught and I like reading about what's going to happen to them." Then she fired off a warning. "So get it right. I don't want people coming into my boutique telling me my son got something wrong."

She was kidding, of course.

No, she wasn't. If there was one thing on earth that Mom did not kid around about, it was the customers who shopped at her store. Business was only as good as the last day's receipts, or so she liked to say, a lot, especially when she was in a bad mood or one of the big outfits in the city was having a sale.

The break lasted twenty minutes. I did nothing for most of it. I stuck my head in the courtroom once and saw that it was about half full, which meant that it would be about two-thirds full when all the people who were outside having a smoke returned to their seats.

I kept an eye out for Rufus, but I didn't see him anywhere.

Just before I went in to find a seat, I decided to check the docket one more time, and that was when I saw her name, sitting right there in front of me, printed in the same size letters as all the other names, but leaping out at me as if it was written in bright red neon: Clarissa May Jarvis, impaired driving causing injury.

I froze and burned at the same time. My legs went numb. I read it over and over again before it started to sink in. My God, I thought to myself. Clarissa, what have you done?

Then I became aware that someone was talking to me.

"We're going in now," I heard a woman say.

I looked up from the docket and saw an impatient-looking woman staring at me as if I had something seriously wrong with my head, which I took to mean that she had been trying to get my attention for at least a few minutes.

"Pardon me?" I said.

"I said we're going in now. The break's over. The judge is going in."

She turned and went into the courtroom. I stood for a

moment, and then I walked in and took a seat along the back row, in the farthest, deepest corner from the front, and pulled out my notepad.

I wrote down Court, Thursday, October 5 at the top of a page and closed my eyes to think.

Thank God, she wasn't there.

Her lawyer put in an appearance for her. He was a small man with glasses and a shiny bald head. He entered a plea of not guilty and suggested a trial date for sometime in November.

The prosecutor indicated that it was fine with him.

A trial date was set for November 24.

Then, as if nothing at all had just happened, they moved on to the next case. I saw Clarissa's lawyer packing up to leave, so I stuffed my notepad and pen into my backpack and went outside to wait for him.

His name was Wayne Toomy. He did not know Clarissa and I were related until I told him.

"No kidding?" he said, looking more amused than concerned. "Your old man's running for mayor out here, isn't he?"

I nodded. "He sure is."

Toomy made a face. "I hate politics."

He told me everything I wanted to know. On the night of Friday, September 29, Clarissa was involved in a traffic accident on the highway leading from Edmonton to Emville. Apparently she had run another car off the road as she was trying to make a right-hand turn into town.

"How do you run a car off the road turning right?" I said.

"She was in the left lane," said Toomy.

I closed my eyes and started to rub my forehead. I remembered when Clarissa had announced to the family, with great pride and arrogance, that she had stopped accepting clients charged with drunk driving offences because she was sick to death of listening to their lies and excuses.

Now she was one of them.

"And she's pleading not guilty?" I said.

Toomy shrugged. "She knows your dad's election is October 20, so she wanted me to try and have it moved back a bit. But you always plead not guilty to these sorts of things. Cops make mistakes. Files get misplaced. Witnesses don't show up. Going to trial is the only chance she has."

I thought about that for a moment. "So, if no one says anything about this until November, what happens?"

"Well, if no one says anything, then no one will know about it, and your dad can win or lose the election on his own. Without her help, if you know what I mean."

I looked up to the sky for a moment and rubbed the back of my neck. I had just gone from being very excited about being at the courthouse, to wishing I was anywhere else in the world.

"What are you doing here anyway?" said Toomy, paying some actual attention to me for the first time. "She told me nobody in her family knew about this."

I told him what I was doing.

"So you're a reporter?" he said.

"Yes."

"And you're here on assignment?"

"Yes."

"Covering the courthouse."

"Yes."

He took a deep breath and thought for a moment. "Well, so much for keeping it a secret."

I shrugged. "I didn't know she was going to be here."

"That was the point of keeping it quiet," said Toomy. "That's what a secret is. You don't tell people."

I was going to say, "I know that," but I decided not to.

"So, are you gonna write about this in the paper, then?" he said.

I looked at him for a moment, then I looked away. The thought had crossed my mind that if no one else knew about the charge against Clarissa, I could probably wait until her case went to trial, which would be well after the election.

But that wouldn't exactly be sticking with the journalist's code of ethics, now would it? Not that there is such a thing as a journalist's code of ethics. I've watched enough TV to know that. But still. And what if Kip somehow found out about it? What if someone in the courtroom tipped him off? Where would that leave me? And why would I do such a thing anyway? For Dad? He hadn't done anything wrong. For Clarissa? Her day was coming whether I wrote about her in the paper or not. For me? I hadn't done anything wrong. I wasn't the one with a date with the judge.

"I don't know," I said, keeping my doors open.

"Well, get it right if you do, my friend," said Toomy, as he turned to leave. "Your whole family's gonna feel this, so don't screw it up."

"How do you mean?" I said.

"I mean Clarissa did not resist arrest. She has spent no time in jail. The injuries she caused were not serious. So don't make her out to be some serial killer in a car. And you want to hear something else? The guy she cut off was going 160 kilometers an hour. He ended up about two hundred yards into some farmer's field beside the highway."

"So?" I said. What difference did any of that make? She was the one who got her lanes mixed up.

"So you better be good," Toomy said, pointing his finger at me as he walked away. "You better be very good."

I watched him cross the parking lot. His threat was not making me feel any better.

"Very good at what?" said a voice beside me. I didn't even have to look to see who it was.

Once again, his timing was perfect.

"Handball," I said. It was the first thing that came to my mind, and I have no idea why, because I don't think I had played handball two times in my entire life. But there was no way I was going to tell Rufus about Clarissa.

"Handball?" he said.

"Yes. It's a sport you play with your hand. And a ball."

Rufus looked after Toomy. "Why does that guy care if you're any good at handball?"

"I'm playing him tomorrow night."

"You are?"

"Yes."

"How do you know him?"

"He's a friend of my sister."

Rufus kept his eyes on Toomy. "He looks like a lawyer."

"He is a lawyer. And this is the courthouse."

"Is your sister a lawyer?"

"Yes."

He turned and looked at me. "Is she cute?"

I returned his stare. He was in the process of lighting another cigarette.

"Is she what?" I said.

He lit his smoke and waved out the match. "You heard me. I asked if your sister was cute."

"Why?"

"Because I've always wanted to date a lawyer, that's why. I find that whole profession to be very sexy."

"Sexy?"

"Yes. All these women standing there, all dressed up, stating their cases and arguing with the judge."

"You think that's sexy? A woman arguing with a judge?"

"I think it beats answering a telephone, I can tell you that. Or carrying around a bedpan from room to room in a hospital."

"I don't think nurses carry bedpans around from room to room."

"You get the picture. They do a lot of unattractive things, that's all I'm saying. Things that you would never, ever see a lawyer doing. Lawyers have their own briefcases and those snappy little cell phones. And they're all stinkin' rich."

"Yes," I said, "but Rufus, you're forgetting one thing."

"What's that?"

"You're sixteen years old."

"So?"

"So don't you think you're a bit young to be dating a lawyer?"

"No. I'm too young to date a doctor. But I do know one I'm keeping my eyes on. She's a very foxy lady. But lawyers. They don't have to go to school for an extra ten years or anything. You can be a lawyer at twenty-three, twenty-four."

"And you think you could get a date with a twenty-three-year-old?"

"Why not?"

I looked away. I had bigger things to think about than Rufus's conquests as a male animal, but I had to admit, I would love to see him ask a twenty-three-year-old lawyer out for a date.

"I don't know," I said. "Maybe you're right."

"Of course I'm right. You should try it. We could double."

"That would not be good," I said, trying to not even think about going out on a date with Rufus.

"Why not?"

I shook my head. It was time for me to leave again, or for him to leave again, and for me to think about how I was going to manage this story I had just walked into.

"Why not?" he said.

I was too distracted to give him an answer.

"Hey," he said, to get my attention. Then he gave up

on it. "Come on. Let's go inside and see if anything's going on. I'll show you a trick so you don't have to sit through every boring thing that goes on in there."

I followed him back into the courthouse. I had no idea why I was returning, but I did know that he wouldn't find out about Clarissa, since her case had already come and gone.

He walked over to the same counter I had been standing at and picked up the court docket.

"Ever seen one of these?" he said.

"Yes."

"It's a list of all the names and cases before the court."

"I said yes."

"All you have to do is go through it, and if there's nothing here that's interesting, you blow."

"I know that," I said, and then I saw him flip the pages of the docket back to the beginning and proceed to go down the row after row of names and charges. My heart stopped beating. If he got a hold of Clarissa's story he would turn it into the scandal of the century, and Dad's chances of winning the election would be as high as his chances of becoming the next president of the United States.

He finished page one and started on two. Her name was halfway down the second page. I followed his finger as it moved down the row. He was two away from her. Then one. Then...

"Hey," he said, stopping. "This one sounds good. Drunk driving causing injury."

I moved over to make it look good. My whole body was stiff with fear.

"Ah damn, she's from Edmonton," said Rufus, moving his finger to where it listed the person's name and address. "Clarissa May Jarvis," he said. "You know her?"

I couldn't speak.

"Probably not," he said. "Probably some city slicker coming into town for a good time with the country boys. Except she got drunk on the way out and ran some poor slob off the road."

I moved my lips but I did not make a sound.

"Oh, well. Her case is long gone now."

He moved down the list. I sagged right beside him with relief. In fact, I nearly put my hand on his shoulder for support.

A couple of minutes later he pushed the docket aside and turned to leave.

"Let's go, Peanuts. There's nothing here for me. For you, maybe, and all those little court brief things you guys are so proud of. But there's nothing here that'll turn us on."

I walked with him through the doors and outside to the parking lot.

"So, you going home?" he said, his hands stuck deep into his pockets, his notepad jammed under his left arm.

"Yes," I said, breaking my silence.

"I'll see you tomorrow then," he said. "We'll compare notes."

"Sure," I said, but I didn't really mean it.

We walked off in opposite directions, and as soon as he was out of sight, I sat down on the nearest bench I could find and lowered my head into my hands.

When I used to think of how cool it would be to be a reporter for a newspaper, I never thought of anything like this.

< 10 >

I phoned my girlfriend Sunny as soon as I got home. She was the only person in the world I wanted to talk to.

Sunny speaks her mind no matter who she's talking to or what she's talking about. She's honest without being mean, and tactful without watering down what she's trying to say.

I could spend three hours talking about how much I miss her, but that would be, as she would put it, a waste of three hours, since no amount of whining was going to get her back before her art course was finished.

She answered the phone on the third ring and said, "Oh, God," when I told her what had happened at the courthouse. For a moment after she said that, I felt that maybe I had called the wrong person, that I was on the hot seat of *Millionaire*, and I had just phoned a friend for help on the million-dollar question, and after giving her all four possible answers — or two if I had gone for the fifty-fifty first, which I have always thought was good strategy — she had said, "Oh, God," which essentially meant that I had made a mistake phoning her instead of someone else, and it was time to take a walk.

"Don't say 'Oh, God,' anymore," I said.

"Why not?" said Sunny.

"Because. I need to hear something more than that. I'm feeling a bit 'Oh, God,' myself, and I'm trying to get out of it."

"Well, let me make my tea first then."

I rolled my eyes. I had caught her at tea time.

Sunny had a ritual of making herself a pot of tea every night. It could be herbal or chai, whichever was available, and nothing, absolutely nothing, including a desperation long-distance call from her boyfriend, could interrupt or delay it. "Can you give me a minute?"

I waited for her to make her tea.

She came back a few moments later. I could hear the soft clink of her cup and saucer as she sat down. I could see her now, too, even though I couldn't, really. She was probably wearing her robe, or an old pair of blue jeans and a T-shirt. Her long, brown hair would be wet, because she likes to wash it every night. Her skin would be soft and clean and cool. Sunny had the coolest skin in the world, and I just loved to touch it. "So, I can't say 'Oh, God,' anymore," she said. "Got it."

My anxiety, which had vanished completely when I was thinking of her curled up in her chair, returned immediately. "I don't even know what I'm so worried about," I said. "It's not like it was me swerving all over the road."

"No, but she is your sister," said Sunny, taking a sip.

"I understand that part of it."

"And even though she just did something incredibly stupid, you still care for her."

"Yes, I do," I said. Actually, I cared for her more now than I ever had in my entire life, which was sort of ironic.

"And she's in huge trouble."

I felt my stomach drop when Sunny said that.

Every time I thought of someone being in trouble, I thought of a little kid standing in front of a big, raging principal with his fist way up in the air and his face turning as red as fresh blood. I did not like having that picture in my head, but as I talked to Sunny on the phone, the little kid became Clarissa and the principal became a judge, who, I happen to know, belongs to a profession that can look even uglier than principals when they get mad.

"I mean, you can't go around running people off the highway without having something happen to you," Sunny went on.

"I know that," I said.

"So she's going to lose her license for sure. And she might lose her job. She might lose her family."

I was silent for a moment. "She's not going to lose her family over this," I said, but it was almost more like a question than a statement, and it would have been a question if I had added "Is she?" at the end of it, which I came close to doing.

"I wouldn't be so sure," said Sunny. "Some people get pretty upset when their husband or wife goes out and does something really stupid and dangerous. I know I would."

I would too, I said to myself. And Michael had been showing signs of frustration with Clarissa even before this happened.

"I know your mom wouldn't be too terribly impressed with your dad if he did something like that."

I closed my eyes. I couldn't even begin to think about what that would look like.

"So it's not out of the question."

"No, it's probably not," I said.

"But you know what, Harper? That shouldn't be any of your concern anyway. Clarissa's a big girl. She's old enough to be held accountable for the decisions she makes. You should have nothing to be worried about."

"I just said that."

"It's your sister who has something to be worried about."

"I know."

"She's the one who got into her car and went out for a drive when she had no business being anywhere but in bed, or in a bar somewhere, passed out on the counter."

"I've said that to myself a million times."

"All you've done is your job."

"I know."

"You did what Kip sent you over there for."

At the mention of the word Kip, my breathing became tight and my palms started to sweat as if I'd just sat down in a steam room.

I already knew that if I had arrived at the courthouse five minutes after the break, this whole business with Clarissa would have been done and gone without me having any knowledge of it, and I would have walked in and sat in the back and written about all the other people who had problems with the law. Would I have checked the docket before leaving? I don't know. Maybe I would have. Maybe I wouldn't. Maybe I would have discovered her name with Rufus — wouldn't that have been interesting.

On the other hand, maybe I would have said hi and goodbye to Rufus on my way out of court, and that would have been the end of it.

And if Kip had found out about it later, my answer to him would have been an honest one: I didn't know anything about it.

But I arrived just before the break, so I had lots of time to check the docket not once, but twice, to make sure I saw it, and now I had this stupid story burning a hole in my notepad: Candidate's Daughter Charged After Accident: Alcohol a factor, say police.

Suddenly, I knew what was bugging me.

"I know what's bugging me," I said.

"What is it?" said Sunny.

"Kip."

"Kip?"

"Yes."

"Why Kip?"

I took in a deep breath. "Because he hates my dad's guts and I think he'd love to get back at him, and running this story about Clarissa on the front page would be a pretty good way of doing it."

Sunny was silent. "He hates your dad's guts?"

"Yes."

"Since when?"

"And you know what? If she got drunk and got in behind the wheel of her car and tried to turn right from the left lane out here on the 401, you'd be arranging her funeral right now, not her next court date. So keep it in perspective. People are killed by drunk drivers every day. Clarissa is getting off easy, and so is everybody else in your family."

She was right about that, too.

"I mean, this whole thing, Harper, it's not about your dad running for mayor, or you passing some stupid test as a reporter. It's about your family, and how all of you are going to respond to a family member in need. That's what it's about."

I had to think about that for a second. "That means I blew it the other night, when she was over at the house."

"No, it doesn't."

"Yes, it does."

"No, it doesn't."

"Sure it does."

"You probably saved her that night by making sure she didn't drive home by herself."

"I didn't save her. I dragged her into bed," I said. I was in no mood to be called a hero.

"Well, maybe if there'd been someone around to drag her into bed the other night, this whole mess wouldn't be happening," said Sunny.

I took a deep breath and stayed reclined in my chair. Mom would have called it slouching, and if she had walked in and seen me, she would have told me to sit up before my spine stays like that for the rest of my life, but under the circumstances, I found it to be a remarkably comfortable way to sit.

"Anyway, can we talk about something else now?" said Sunny. "I know it's important and everything, but we talk, like, once a week to each other."

I closed my eyes and tried to think. For the past two hours, every second of my life had been spent thinking about Clarissa and Dad and Kip, with a dash of Rufus on the side, especially when he was reading down the docket.

"Sure," I said. "I could use a break from it, too, actually."

"Well then. Have you done anything else exciting this week, other than reporting on the self-destruction of your sister?"

"I got drunk two nights ago," I said, quite matter-of-factly, as if I had gotten drunk last week as well, and the week before.

"You what?" said Sunny.

"I got drunk two nights ago. On whisky. In Kip's office."

"Oh, terrific," said Sunny. "What is this, a family theme you guys are working on?"

"No. But I think I talked too much."

"Why do you say that?"

"I just do. I think I got a little light in the head and started yapping about things I probably shouldn't have been yapping about."

"Well, that's kind of what being drunk is all about, isn't it?" said Sunny. "Isn't talking too much something that you're supposed to do?"

"I don't know. I just know I did it."

"How do you know that?"

"I just do."

"Well, what did you talk about?"

I hesitated. "Your bras."

"My what?"

"And the covers on those little boxes in the ladies' underwear section of the department stores."

"What about them?"

"I used to like looking at them when I went shopping with my mom."

Sunny was silent for a moment. "That's sick, Harper."

"No, it's not."

"I think it is."

"Well, it's not."

"I wish I had known this about you when we first met."

"Well, if we had met in a department store instead of a writing camp, you might have. Dixie says buy the bra, by the way."

"Buy the what?"

"Buy the bra. The liquid-lift? She says go for it."

"I'm not buying a liquid-lift bra."

"You're not?"

"No."

"How come?"

"Because I don't need one."

"I thought you did."

"Who told you that?"

"Mom."

"Your mother told you I needed a liquid-lift bra?"

There was a slight bit of tension in Sunny's voice.

"No. She told me that the two of you talked about them the last time you called me."

I could practically see Sunny shaking her head. "Well, I'm glad she shared that with you. It's so nice to see that the lines of communication are wide open over there all of a sudden."

"Why don't you think you need one?" I said. It was fun talking about this with her.

"It's not a question of need, Harper. I just don't want one. Your mom happened to mention them and we fell into a conversation. I've never thought of buying a liquid-lift bra in my life."

"Dixie says they really enhance the look."

Sunny sighed. "I'll remember that the next time I go shopping."

"Can I come with you?"

"Not on your life. You'd make me jealous of all the boxes you'd be gawking at."

"Oh, come on."

"Forget it."

"You know, with a liquid-lift bra, you could probably be on one of those boxes yourself."

"Wow. What a thrill that would be."

"It would."

"You could take pictures of me and put them on every box in your house."

"I could blow them up to poster size."

"Yes, you could."

"So, how about it?" I said. I was having so much fun kidding with her.

"How about you find me a five-leaf clover and the pot of gold at the end of the rainbow, and then we'll talk about getting me some kind of special-effects bra."

"Mom thinks you're pretty terrific, by the way," I said. I felt it was time to stick that in.

"Oh, does she?"

"Yes."

"Well, isn't that nice."

"She thinks you're a wonderful girl."

"Well, I'm glad to hear that."

"So does Dixie."

"Really."

"I told her all about you."

"And who else did you tell all about me? Or did you just have this conversation about bras with Dixie while the two of you were alone?"

"No, no. Kip and Tom were there, too."

"I figured they were. For some reason."

"But we were all very mature about it."

"I bet you were."

"Except Tom. He heard what I had to say, then he told us all about the underwear he was wearing."

"Well, that was nice of him."

"Actually, it wasn't."

"And what kind was he wearing, in case I go shopping for my brother sometime soon? Or you, for that matter, since we're getting to be so intimate with each other."

"I don't know. But it rode up a lot when he was driving in his car. I guess it was quite a distraction."

I could see Sunny frown over the phone. "I don't think I had to hear that."

"That's what I'm talking about. It was not a pleasant experience."

"In fact, I think I should probably go now. It's very late here."

"I'm just getting to the good stuff. We talked about themes and patterns."

"Goodbye, Harper," said Sunny. "Good luck with your story. Call me tomorrow after you talk with Kip if you'd like."

I said goodbye and I-love-you, even though Mom thinks we're too young to be in love, and hung up. I imagined Sunny staying in her chair for a few minutes and finishing off her tea. Perhaps she would get up to get herself a second cup, or maybe she would just sit for awhile and think about our conversation, or about something else going on in her life.

As for me, I got back to worrying as much as I had before I talked with her.

By the time I went to bed, Mom and Dad were still out. I tried phoning Clarissa, just for the heck of it, but there was no answer there, either.

< 11 >

Kip and I ended up writing the story about Clarissa together. It ran the following Tuesday on the front page
with the headline, "Mayoral Candidate's Drunk Daughter Causes Crash." As a kicker, Kip put on top of the
headline, in italics, *Trial date set for after the election.*
It started off like this:

*The daughter of longtime town councilor and
current mayoral candidate, Dr. Benjamin Winslow,
was charged last Thursday with one count of drunk
driving causing injury.*

*The charge stems from an accident on Septem-
ber 27. Driving north on Highway 47 at
approximately 11:30 pm, Clarissa May Jarvis, 33,
who currently lives in Edmonton but was born,
raised, and educated in Emville, allegedly at-
tempted to make a right-hand turn from the
left-hand lane at the Emville turn-off.*

Driving behind Ms. Jarvis was Dwight Lesbon,

also of Edmonton, whose car was forced off the road, through the ditch on the east side of the highway, and into an adjacent farmer's field.

Mr. Lesbon suffered a broken wrist and minor head lacerations in the accident. His car, a 2000 Ford Taurus, was badly damaged.

Ms. Jarvis entered a plea of not guilty and will await trial on November 24, nearly one month after the completion of the municipal elections.

Her father, who has served on Emville's town council since 1972, has been considered by some to be the frontrunner in the current race for mayor.

In a brief interview, Dr. Winslow said that the family offers its wishes for a speedy recovery to Mr. Lesbon and will await the outcome of the trial before making any further comments.

Dr. Winslow also indicated that the family was not aware that their daughter had ever driven while intoxicated before, but will stand behind her regardless of the trial's outcome.

The Winslow family has been a cornerstone in the community for years.

Kip had gone on and on with this part of it. I think he wanted to make sure that everyone who even just glanced at the piece knew who he was writing about. My contributions were really just sitting there telling him everything that Mom and Dad had ever done or won since they moved to Emville, and when Clarissa went to school.

It seemed like everyone in town read it. Mom had the busiest day of her life at her store. Not the best, mind you, from a sales perspective, which is the only perspective she's interested in, but the busiest, with half the town dropping by to see how she was doing. The other half left messages on our answering machine at home.

Dad took calls at his clinic for the first half of the day, then decided to hell with it and spent the afternoon at the golf course. It was a very warm, mid-autumn day, so he wasn't the only person out there, but he didn't exactly have to wait long for a tee time, either.

For me, the day was pretty quiet. A couple of teachers raised their eyebrows and said that they'd seen the piece in the paper. Mrs. Button, the vice-principal, told me I had a lot of guts, which I appreciated, although I'm not sure if she was paying me a compliment or telling me I was crazy.

At the end of the day I ran into Rufus. He was by himself, leaning against the fence that runs alongside the track, smoking a cigarette. He waved me over when he saw me.

"Peanuts," he said, extending his hand for a handshake. "Congratulations."

"For what?" I said, shaking his hand.

"That was a helluva scoop you laid on me," he said. "A helluva scoop. I underestimated you. You're sleazier than I thought."

"Thanks," I said.

"Hey, that's a compliment. In this business, that's like telling a runway model her legs are longer than you first thought, or a running back he's three seconds faster than anyone knew."

"I'm touched," I said.

"You should be. You got the big triple crown all in one story. You lied to me. You ratted on your sister. And you screwed your dad's chances of ever winning the election. That's amazing. I've never heard of that happening with one story before. And you're all family."

I took in a deep breath. Outside of Kip and Dixie and everyone else at work, and Sunny, but she was a bit far away to help me at the moment, this had been the dominant reaction to Clarissa's story: how could a brother do such a thing to his own sister, and a son do that to his dad?

I even heard a rumor that a reporter with *The Globe & Mail* had been trying to contact me to follow up on the whole family-angle thing. I don't know if it was true or not, but just the rumor that there was a rumor was enough to make my knees go weak.

"Rufus, I wrote a news story, okay? I can't help who was in it. I'm sorry I lied to you, but I couldn't help it. And I didn't screw my dad's chances of winning the election. Clarissa did."

Rufus took a deep pull on his smoke. "Okay, Peanuts. No need to get defensive. What she did was very stupid, I'll grant you that. You should never turn right from the left-hand lane. Drunk or not, it's a dumb thing to do and you're asking for trouble. Especially on the highway. But then she got smart. She started thinking like a lawyer, pleading not guilty and all that, to push the date back, and I've told you before, I find that profession to be very sexy. Nice picture of her too, by the way. She looks like someone I might want to call later. See how she's doing."

I said nothing. The picture he was referring to was

lifted, by me, from one of the family photo albums Mom and Dad have in their closet. Mom was not happy when she saw it in the newspaper. She wasn't exactly singing songs from *The Sound of Music* before that, mind you, not with everything that was going on, but she was really ticked when she saw that picture.

"You have a lot of nerve, young man," she had said, her hands on her hips, wishing, I would imagine, that she had a holster with a pair of six-shooters right there by her fingertips, so she could put an end to this "business," as she called it, before it got any worse.

"Kip asked for a picture," I said. It was the only defense I had, and I knew it was going to cause trouble, but at the time I took it, it had made sense to run a picture of Clarissa along with the story, and as Paula (of all people) had pointed out, I was the only one who had direct access to one.

"I don't care what he asked for. What if he had asked you for a blood sample? What would you have done? Gone after her with a needle?"

"No."

"He is your employer," she went on. "Not your keeper. You do not have to do everything he tells you to do."

"I realize that," I said, although I don't think I really did.

"So what are you doing it for then? What are you sneaking around, taking pictures out of family photo albums to take to the newspaper for?"

"I wasn't sneaking around," I said, trying mightily to hold my ground.

"Well, you weren't exactly walking through the front door asking me if I knew of any pictures of Clarissa you could use for the paper, now were you?"

She got me on that one. I still haven't thought of a comeback for it.

"What's her phone number, anyway?" said Rufus, as we moved away from the fence and started to walk towards the sidewalk.

"I'm not going to give you my sister's phone number," I said.

"Why not?"

"Because."

"Because why?"

"Because I'm not stupid, that's why."

Rufus gave me a funny look. "What are you changing the subject for?"

"What?"

"We're not talking about your intellect. We're talking about your sister. If you want to talk about your intellect, fine. Let's discuss it. Let's talk about the wisdom of a guy who brings his own family's laundry to the table, dumps it all out for everyone to see, then picks out a few particularly stained pieces and waves them to the crowd in case they missed them. Let's talk about that if you want. But all I was after was your sister's lousy phone number."

"Well, forget it," I said.

"Then let's talk about your intellect."

"No."

"Why not?"

"We just did."

"When?"

"You said I was lousy with laundry. Maybe you're right. Maybe I should have just left the whole thing alone."

Mom and Dad's reaction to the piece had actually been pretty mild compared to Clarissa's.

I had called her last Friday morning, the day after I had been at the courthouse, to tell her that I knew about the charge against her, and that I would be doing a story on her for the next edition of the paper.

She was not impressed, nor was she the sad, lonely, pitiful thing that had gotten plastered in our kitchen just a couple of weeks before, which was actually fortunate for me, because she was quite likeable that way.

"You're what?" she had said.

I repeated myself. "I'm a reporter, remember. I'm doing a story about you and this drunk driving thing."

She was silent.

"I have all the facts. I'm just calling to let you know. I think you should call Mom and Dad and tell them."

"Tell them what?" she had said, her voice turning to ice. "That their daughter was in an accident, or that you're about to ruin any chance Dad has of becoming mayor? Because let me tell you something, little brother. You do not have to do this. So what if you know about my accident now? Nothing's been proven. I'm innocent until proven guilty, not the other way around. Have you not heard of that before?"

I repeated, once again, what I was doing. "I was at the courthouse, Clarissa. I saw that you'd been charged. It's my obligation to report it."

She took a deep breath over the phone. "Harper, get

your head out of the clouds. You're not writing for the *New York Times* or the *Washington Post* or any of those other newspapers you fantasize over. You're a work experience student learning your so-called trade. You're not under any obligation of any kind to do anything except show up and collect your credits."

"Sure I am."

"No, you're not."

"Of course I am."

She changed her tack. "Are you?"

"Yes."

"Then tell me. How much is this guy paying you to be a reporter?"

I hesitated before answering. "He's not paying me anything. He's giving me experience."

"Oh, is that how it works?"

"Yes."

"So he's counting on you to fulfill all of your obligations as a reporter, while he violates the number one obligation of an employer, which is to provide financial compensation to his employees for the work they do."

"How do you know that?"

"Because first of all, I was a naive little work experience student myself many years ago, so I know all about the just-be-thankful-for-the-opportunity routine, and second of all, the line of work you're in isn't exactly famous for treating its people well. In fact, it sucks, to coin a phrase of a client of mine who used to be in the business. So get with it."

This was only just the beginning. She shifted gears again and tried to become my buddy.

"Now listen to me, Harper," she said, her voice softening. "I know you're just trying to do your job. That's very honorable of you. I'm sure you're the best student reporter that guy has had in there in years. But I'm not telling you to throw the story in the garbage or pretend it never happened. I'm asking you to wait until it's a more appropriate time to print it. That's all I'm asking, and you can do that. It's well within your 'obligation' as a reporter."

I had been all set to agree with her. I could feel the relief pouring into my body like fresh air through an open window. God, I felt good. But she had kept talking, about Dad and his desire to become mayor, and Mom because it was about time she and Dad got the respect they deserved, and I started to think, What is Clarissa talking about? Dad has not spent his entire life dreaming of becoming a mayor. He was doing this almost as a favor to the outgoing Mayor Harrison. And Mom had never said anything about wanting more respect. She wanted more time to sleep, not respect.

So I called Clarissa on it. I asked her point-blank what her real reason was for wanting me to hold off on the story, and she said nothing. She told me she was telling the truth, and when I told her that I didn't believe her, she hung up on me.

I called her back and told her she had until Saturday morning to tell Mom and Dad. After that, I would tell them, or they would just find out like everyone else in town on Tuesday.

So she called them. And then Kip called Dad. Then my brother William called from Ontario, for no good reason other than "to chat," as he liked to put it, and Mom told him everything.

On Saturday night we had ourselves a little show-down, so to speak, where we all presented our cases, except William, who sent his by email but no one remembered to check it, except me, but I decided to join the others and forget about it.

Mom said she thought this whole work experience thing was getting way out of hand and should be stopped immediately. Dad said there was no place for malice in journalism, and that Kip should be taught a lesson in responsible reporting practices. "Didn't you walk in here just the other day and comment on how much drinking takes place at your office?" he said to me. "Do you think a person who keeps a bottle of whisky in his desk drawer has any right to point a finger at someone else?" Clarissa said the same tired old thing she had used on me the day before. And I told them that as far as I could see, it was simple: Clarissa's name was on the docket, her case was presented to the court, and a trial date was set. That's the story, and it should be printed.

Miraculously enough, I won.

But that didn't mean they were happy with it. On Sunday, Dad told me on his way to church (where he practically never goes) to be bloody careful with anything I put in the paper. Mom asked if she could see a copy of the story before it went to press. I said no, we don't do that kind of thing. That hadn't been the answer she was looking for, but she didn't fight it.

Clarissa still had not said another word to me.

Then, of course, the story came out and Mom blew a

gasket over the photograph I swiped. At least I took a good one, was something else I could have said. But luckily, I didn't.

"You really think so?" said Rufus, as we continued towards downtown Emville. I wasn't sure where he was going, but I was heading to the office to get ready for tomorrow night's debate. "You think you should have just left the story sitting there?"

I thought about it some more. "Probably not."

Rufus nodded. "Good answer, Peanuts. I have faith in you now. Don't make me lose it."

"Faith in me for what?"

"Faith in you that you can carry the torch when I leave. That the townspeople will be in good hands with you as their watchdog."

"Where are you going?" I said.

"Nowhere if I get scooped like that again," said Rufus. He stopped walking to light a new cigarette. Then he turned to begin walking in a new direction. "But I would like to leave this place behind someday, and I am rapidly running out of chances to land a job at a daily with this election."

"Meaning what?" I said. I really had no idea what he was talking about.

"Meaning you might be sleazier than I thought, but you're still no match for me," he said. "So watch out tomorrow."

He turned and left me standing there on the street. For a moment, I wondered what he might be up to. Then it passed, and I walked on without thinking about it again.

< 12 >

Mom and Dad went out for supper before the debate. They left the house at around five-thirty, meaning they missed another visit with Clarissa by about ten minutes.

They were quite relaxed when they left. They were going out with some friends to The Steakhouse, Mom's favorite restaurant in town, and then heading over to the school gym for seven-fifteen. The debate was set to begin at seven-thirty.

Dad was looking very polished and confident and ready "to get it on," as he liked to say, on occasion, when he was feeling particularly macho.

Mom was looking very poised, which was, to her, what the spouse of every candidate in any election should look like.

Neither of them said too much about how they thought the night might go, but I think they were hoping it would go pretty well.

Clarissa was looking neither polished, confident, nor poised when she came into the house. I was in the kitchen making a grilled cheese sandwich for supper. I had the sandwich maker plugged in and was waiting for it to heat up when I heard the front door open and then close. I figured it was Mom or Dad running back to pick something up, so that's why I jumped nearly two feet in the air when Clarissa stuck her smiling face around the corner and said, in a pretty loud voice, "Boo!"

I even dropped the sandwich flipper on the floor.

"Scared you, didn't I?" she said, her eyes wide. "I can be pretty light on my feet when I wanna be."

I watched her walk into the kitchen and drop her purse on the table. She was wearing a pair of old gray sweatpants and a white T-shirt and bare feet. Not exactly standard fare for her.

She flopped into a chair and looked at me and smiled again.

"Smells good, whatever you're making."

"It's a grilled cheese sandwich," I said, cautiously, as I tried to figure out which Clarissa I was about to spend time with: either the relatively pleasant, albeit very drunk, one I spent a night in the kitchen with a few weeks ago, or the severe, razor-sharp one I had tangled with over the telephone.

"Can I have a bite?" she said.

"A bite?"

"Yes. Just a little one. With some ketchup, if you don't mind."

I thought for a moment. I think I had my answer. "I can make you a whole one, if you want."

Clarissa reached into her purse and pulled out a pack of cigarettes, matches, and several small pill containers that rattled as she put them down. Then she stared at the clock on the wall across from her and made a calculation.

"Are you sure?" she said, glancing at me.

"I think I can handle it."

"Do you have any pickles?"

"I believe so."

"Dill pickles?"

"Yes."

She thought for another moment. "Okay. I'll have one." She looked again at the clock. "I can eat in fifteen minutes. After that, I can't eat again until ten, and then I can't go to sleep until twelve, because my final pill of the day comes two hours after my last meal, which must be no sooner than four hours after my previous pill, or else it will spoil the effectiveness of the medication." She shook her head and stared at everything on the table. "God, what a lot to remember, and on a night like tonight to boot. How's Dad?"

"He's fine," I said, lifting my sandwich to a plate.

"And Mom?"

I shrugged my shoulders. I wanted to ask her about all the medication she was on, but she wasn't giving me much of a chance to. "She's okay."

"Good," said Clarissa, with another smile. "I'm glad to hear that."

I handed her the sandwich and began buttering some bread for another one.

"That's wonderful," said Clarissa, going on about Mom and Dad. "I'm glad to hear they're doing so well. And thank you so much for the sandwich. That was very kind of you."

I put the butter knife down and leaned against the counter with my arms crossed and looked at her. "Clarissa," I said. "What's going on?"

She frowned. "What do you mean?"

"I mean with you. What's going on?"

"What makes you think anything's going on?"

I gave her a look. "You walk in here and say boo. Then you thank me very much for a sandwich that has butter on both sides of the bread and a thick hunk of cheese in the middle of it? A month ago you would have called 911 to report a suicide by cholesterol in progress. You don't think that's reason enough to ask you what's going on?"

She smiled again. It was a big, happy, glowing smile. "It's the new me, Harper. I'm happier, leaner, more re-laxed."

"What's with the cigarettes?"

"I've taken up smoking."

"Why?"

"Because I felt like it. It's something I've never done before. And besides, why not?"

"Because they're no good for you."

"They've helped me lose weight."

"What weight? You don't weigh anything."

"I sure do. You should have seen my rear end at Christmas time. It was disgusting. I stood in front of the mirror every night for a month, bare naked, looking at my fat behind."

"You don't have a behind."

"It was depressing."

"You could look at your behind with one of those

little compact mirrors you carry in your purse."

"I can now, you mean. But anyway, I'm not worried about that anymore. That's not going to bother me. You know why?"

"Tell me."

"One word."

"What is it?"

"Oprah."

"What?"

"I picked up my first copy of her magazine the other day in the doctor's office and I can honestly say, it's changed my life. 'How To Be Happy' was the name of one of the stories. Can you believe it? There I am, sitting in a waiting room full of losers waiting for my prescriptions to be refilled, and this story jumps out at me. I could not stop talking about it when my doctor called me in. 'That Oprah,' I kept saying to her. 'Why didn't I think of her before?'"

"What did your doctor say?"

Clarissa shook her head. "She's not a believer. She is where I was last week. But I'm going to work on her. Just watch. She'll be eating the same foods and reading the same books as me in no time. It will not take long. I told her, I said this to her myself, I said, 'You're as unhappy as I was. I can see it in the bags under your eyes, and the way your shoulders sag when you think no one's looking.' I notice these things, you know. It's my job as a lawyer to pick these things up."

"You said all that to your doctor?"

"I said, 'Read this article. You'll feel a lot better.'"

"What did she say?"

"She said it was the medication."

"What medication?"

"That I'm on. The anti-depressants. The energy pills. The sleeping pills. She said it had nothing to do with the magazine and everything to do with these silly little pills, which I adore, by the way. I call them my little life savers."

I started right then to get very worried. Mom used to tell me that as a kid, Clarissa would run out the door and down the street whenever they tried to give her an Aspirin. Now she was walking around with half a drugstore in her purse.

"How long have you been on those?" I said.

"Well, off and on, for quite some time now, but lately I've been really on them because my life is such a mess. But I've already told that story today, to that buddy of yours. I don't really feel like getting into it again. Now, would you mind getting me a pickle? This sandwich is getting cold, and I love having grilled cheese sandwiches with pickles."

I didn't move. "My buddy?" I said.

"Yes. He phoned me today."

"Who was it?"

"He said he was a friend of yours."

"What did he want?"

Clarissa shrugged her shoulders. "I don't know what he wanted. He wanted to talk to me, that's all I know. I figured you'd know. He's your friend."

"What was his name?"

She shook her head. "I don't know. I have no idea."

"Was it Rufus?"

"Yes."

I briefly closed my eyes. In the pit of my stomach, I started to feel sick.

"Why, what's the matter with that?" said Clarissa.

"Nothing," I said. I saw no reason to tell her who he was. It was too late anyway, and besides, I wasn't sure what kind of story he could do on her at this point. I had already reported on the charge against her.

But at the same time, I knew he was up to something.

"Is this Rufus person not really a friend of yours?" she said.

"Not really."

"What is he then?"

"I don't know."

"Well, is he a gangster?"

"No."

"Does he smuggle things across the border?"

"No."

"Does he trespass on people's lawns and tear up their gardens?"

"He might," I said.

Clarissa finally took a bite of her sandwich. "Would he get me a pickle if I asked him for one, or would he stand there like you and ignore me?"

I turned towards the fridge and got her a giant jar of dill pickles. Then I opened the jar and put the whole thing beside her.

"Thank you," she said, reaching in.

"So you don't remember what he asked you about?" I said.

"No," she said, taking another bite. "Well now. Wait

a minute. I do remember. Of course I remember. He asked me about Dwight."

"Who?"

"Dwight."

"Who's Dwight?"

"The man with the broken wrist."

"The man with the what?"

"The broken wrist." She put her sandwich down. "Do you have anything to drink?"

I stopped to think for a moment. There was something about someone with a broken wrist that sounded familiar, but I could not think of why, or from where.

"Like a glass of milk or something? Or vodka, if you have any. Just a joke. Although I did take a cab today. I doubled up on some of my meds, hence my healthy glow of optimism and good humor."

I wasn't listening to her.

"You're not listening to me, are you, Harper?"

"That's the guy you ran off the road," I said.

"Yes, it is."

"Why were you talking about him?"

"Because he called me today, too, to tell me he's suing me."

"He's what?"

"He's suing me."

"For what? Nothing's even happened yet."

"Well, apparently, lots has happened yet. He's lost his job because he can't be a mechanic if he only has one hand. And he didn't have disability insurance, so he's about to lose his condominium, and the car insurance people won't give him anything until they hear a verdict on the case, which I put off by pleading not guilty because I was about to get a job at the university, teaching law, but I won't get it now because the Dean who was going to hire me happens to live for some ungodly reason on an acreage outside Emville, and so he saw the paper and left a message on my answering machine that regardless of my credentials, which were very impressive, he had no intention of hiring someone charged with drunk driving. Then of course Michael found out, so he promptly packed up the kids and went on a holiday to give me time to figure things out, which is his way of being supportive. The big sweetie. Then of course my own fine employer found out that not only am I about to lose my license, but I was also about to quit my job with them, so they've given me a fine severance package and sent me on my way. So you see, Harper, quite a lot has happened recently, but I know Mom and Dad have been terribly busy the last few days, and I have been reluctant to talk with you about it because I never know how it's going to look the next day in print. But thank God for Oprah. That's all I can say. She's made me feel a whole lot better with one article alone. Now really, can I have something to drink? I am dying of thirst."

"How much of this did you tell Rufus?" I said.

She shrugged her shoulders. "All of it."

"All of it?"

"Yes. Why not?"

"He's a stranger, Clarissa."

"He sounded nice on the phone."

"You don't even know him."

"He likes jazz. He's been to Mexico. We have lots in

common. I had a very enjoyable conversation with him."

"Did he tell you why he wanted to know all of this?"

"Yes."

"Because he's going to write about it in the paper next week."

"That's what he said."

"So why did you do it?" I said. My head was spinning. Rufus, that slimeball, was trying to get my entire family run out of town.

"I just felt like talking," said Clarissa. Then she turned serious. Or as serious as she could, considering the circumstances. "Think about it, Harper. He knew everything before he called. Not about me losing my job and all that, but he knew about Dwight and the lawsuit. He had to. Why else would he have called five minutes after I got off the phone with the other guy? They were working together. Rufus must have tracked him down beforehand and talked with him. For all we know, he was the one who told Dwight to sue me. Or at least threaten to sue me. That's all he's done so far. But my God. All of this has literally just happened."

I rubbed my forehead with my fingers. It was almost too much to take in at once, and I knew right away why Clarissa was taking so many pills. I wasn't even involved in the accident and it was making me feel sick.

"But you know what, Scoop?" she said "It's gonna get worse."

"What is?" I said.

"This whole thing. It's going to get much, much worse."

"How do you know?"

"Because right now Rufus is probably standing in front of a microphone before an audience of about three hundred people, asking Dad questions about a lawsuit he doesn't even know about yet, and about his daughter losing her job, and Dwight's little plight with his broken wrist … and there's nothing anyone can do about it."

I checked the clock on the wall. It was already seven-forty-five, so there was a chance that Rufus actually could be asking Dad questions right now.

I unplugged the sandwich maker and dashed upstairs to get dressed. When I returned to the kitchen, Clarissa was still sitting in the same place, but she was looking extremely tired, as if the full force of her medication had just caught up with her, or as if telling me her story had just drained all her energy.

I said goodbye and ran past her and out the door.

I suppose I could have dragged her off into bed again, but I didn't have time. Plus, I didn't really want to.

< 13 >

I arrived at the school and saw Rufus standing at the end of a long line of people waiting to ask the candidates a question.

I walked up behind him and grabbed him by the arm, the way Mom has been doing to me for the past sixteen years of my life, and asked him to step outside. He hesitated for a moment, then he came with me.

We walked around the corner of the gym and Rufus reached into his jacket pocket and pulled out a cigarette.

"Well, Peanuts," he said, lighting his smoke. "What's up?"

"I know what you're up to, Rufus," I said. "I know what you're going to ask Dad about, and I'm not going to let you."

He did not look terribly surprised. "Oh, no?"

"No."

He blew a row of smoke rings into the air and looked around. "Alright then. Let's make a deal."

"A what?"

"A deal."

"A deal for what?"

He stared at me for a second. "A deal for your sister. Or your dad. However you want to look at it."

He was trying to look cool, like a gangster in one of those old movies.

"What are you talking about?"

"This. I won't walk into that gym and tell everybody about your sister, if you give me your job."

"What?"

"You heard me."

"No, I didn't."

"Yes, you did."

"No. Because it sounded like you just asked to have my job."

"That's right."

"Well, you can't have it."

"Alright. See you inside." He began to walk towards the gym.

"Well, wait a second," I said. He stopped walking and turned around. "Come here."

"No."

"Just for a minute."

"No."

I took a step towards him. "You have to tell me what you're talking about first."

He took another pull on his cigarette. "What I'm talking about is I want your job. What's so hard to understand about that?"

"But you already have a job."

"So what? I want a new one."

"Why?"

"Because I don't like the one I have."

"Why not?"

"Because the people I work with are miserable and my editor's a pig."

"So why did you take it?"

He shrugged. "I want to be a reporter. How else are you supposed to get experience?"

"Why didn't you apply at *The Express*?"

"I did."

"You did not."

"I did so."

"When?"

"Just before you got the job. I was the last guy they interviewed before you."

"You were not."

"Kip even told me I had the job. He just had to interview you first. A formality, he called it. Then he met you and he never called me again. Five times a day I phoned that guy. I left messages on his voice mail at home and the one in his office. I never got a call back. Not one. Then one day I found out that he had hired you, Mr. Pretty-Boy from the school newspaper. Mr. Bug-In-The-Face, or whatever you called that stupid column about the fly."

"It wasn't stupid," I said, getting sidetracked a little.

"Whatever," said Rufus. "It wasn't exactly high art, either."

"Meaning what?" I said. He was talking about the column I used to write called "Fly On The Wall."

"Meaning you impressed Kip with your fancy clothes

and the little stories you submitted, while I went the man's route and talked shop with him for an hour."

"The man's route?" I said.

"That's right."

I hesitated. "Alright. So what? He talked to me and he talked to you, and he chose me. What's so wrong with that?"

"There's everything wrong with it," said Rufus, flinging his smoke to the ground. "I'm the better newsman. I'm the better reporter. But he was looking for someone to do the soft stuff for him. He wasn't looking for a hardball guy. He was looking for someone who could play slo-pitch, and he asked me about it and I said, 'No way. I could never do that. I'd go nuts.' But I was joking. He took me serious."

"How do you know all this?"

"He told me."

"When?"

"Two weeks ago. When I finally caught up with him."

I had to think again. "Well, you're not getting my job."

Rufus smiled. "Alright. Let's go talk to your dad." He turned and started walking towards the gym again.

"Wait," I said.

He stopped.

"Let me think."

He looked at his watch. "Well, hurry up, Peanuts. I haven't got all night."

I had an idea. "Let's call Kip."

"For what?"

"To see what he wants to do. Maybe he'll find work for both of us."

"Maybe he won't," said Rufus.

"Maybe he won't," I said, with a shrug.

"Maybe I should go talk to your dad in the mean-time," said Rufus.

I stared at him. He had such a skinny, wormy face. "Leave my dad alone," I said.

"No problem," said Rufus.

"Promise me that."

"Hand over the keys to the office and I'll be out of his hair forever."

"You will not."

"Or until he decides to run for something again, what-ever comes first."

I was quiet for a moment. Rufus had me and he knew it. But it was such a stupid situation to be in. "You know, Rufus. All you ever had to do is ask me if I want to help you get a job at the paper. You don't have to blackmail me."

"This isn't blackmail."

"Well whatever it is. It feels like blackmail."

"You've been blackmailed before?"

"No."

"Then how would you know?"

I rolled my eyes and took in a deep breath. A differ-ent person would have belted him by now. Tom would have picked him up by his ears and tossed him over the gym. Dixie probably would have pumped him full of holes with pencils and pens and slapped him with a ruler. But me? I was taking the reasonable, gentle approach, and it was getting me nowhere.

Then Paula stepped around the corner and saw us

standing there. Nice, plump Paula, the absolute last person who could help me get out of this jam.

"Harper, who are you talking to?" she said, walking towards us.

I introduced her to Rufus, and vice versa.

"They're taking a break," she said, after they said hi to each other.

"Does Kip know I'm out here?" I said. I was aware that the whole time I was outside with Rufus, I was supposed to be inside interviewing people in the audience about who they thought was winning the debate. It was my assignment for the night, and I wasn't exactly doing it.

"I don't think so," she said. "But he has been looking for you."

"Well, Rufus here has been taking up all of my time," I said. "He wants a job at the paper."

"Our paper?" said Paula.

"Yes," said Rufus, reaching for another cigarette. He was really the picture of health, this guy. What I should have done was just give him my job and watch him slowly smoke himself into the ground. "I want the job he stole from me."

Paula stared at him for a minute. "Harper's never stolen anything in his life," she said, in a tone different than anything I had ever heard her use before.

"Well, he took my job," said Rufus, blowing smoke.

"You can have mine if you get your act together," said Paula.

Rufus and I glanced briefly at each other, then we turned back to her.

"I'm leaving. I got a job at *The Journal*."

"You did?" I said.

"How?" said Rufus.

Paula shrugged. "I'm good at what I do. And I'm not always as nice as people think."

"You're not?" I said.

"No, I'm not."

"When are you not nice?"

"Well, Kip used to go out with my sister, and then he broke up with her, and she was devastated, so I hit him up for a job. I told him it was the least he could do, and he bought it. Then when I started looking around for something else, I got him to write me a letter of reference, and I got him to keep on writing it until he got it right."

"That's pretty clever," said Rufus, who apparently had his own definition of clever.

"I thought so," said Paula.

"What did your sister think?" I said, not that it really mattered.

"She thinks I'm scum," said Paula.

"Scum is good," said Rufus, nodding his head. "Under certain circumstances."

"I think so," said Paula.

"I think so, too," said Rufus, smiling.

"Except when it's in a ring around your bathtub," said Paula. "Ha, ha." They had a laugh over that. I think they were starting to fall in love.

"So what makes you think you can arrange for Rufus to take over your job?" I said.

"Well, when I told Kip I was leaving, he said, 'Find someone.' So …"

"He already knows me, anyway," said Rufus. "He was going to hire me before."

"Well," said Paula, "get in there and do the job. Find out what the people are thinking. I'll tell him you'll have a story for him tomorrow afternoon."

Rufus could barely contain himself. His smile was so wide his yellow teeth looked like a mini crescent moon turned on its side.

"Hey, partner," he said, turning to me. "You take the left side and I'll take the right."

"You don't say anything to my dad," I said.

"About what?" said Paula.

"About nothing," I said. I had no desire to involve any more people in Clarissa's situation.

Rufus, of course, had other ideas. "His sister's being sued by that guy she ran off the road," he said.

"I know that," said Paula.

"You do?" I said.

"Yes. I was down at the courthouse today. One of the cops was talking about it. He said some guy phoned him up and asked him how to file a lawsuit."

Rufus nodded. "That's our boy Dwight. He's not the smoothest tire on the road, I can tell you that. I don't know if he bumped his head when he was driving into the cornfield or what, but he's a pretty dim guy."

"That's what the cop said," said Paula.

"When I talked to him, he didn't even know what a lawsuit was. I think he thought it was the clothes a person puts on to go inside the courthouse."

They had another laugh, and for the second time, I didn't join in. I was feeling sick.

"You mean, you guys know all about this?" I said, meaning Paula and Kip.

"Sure," said Paula, with a shrug.

"Does my dad know?"

"Kip asked him about it. Your dad gave a few comments."

I looked at Rufus. Even he was shaking his head.

"All that work to get a scoop, and that idiot phones the cops to tell them all about it," he said.

I said nothing. I had just spent my entire night trying to keep my family in one piece, and all I had to show for it was a new partner at work, and probably some explaining to do when Kip found out I hadn't done anything.

"So, I will ask your dad about it," said Rufus, giving me a poke. He was having a great time.

"You do that," I said. I stared up at the sky for a moment as Rufus and Paula walked towards the gym, and I wondered how much more of this newspaper business I could take.

< 14 >

Dad eventually lost the election. George Morrison took over as mayor. He ran a quiet campaign, but he was a very solid candidate who had worked for years on various associations and boards.

Whether that had anything to do with why he won will never really be known.

On the day before the election took place, Kip ran the story about the lawsuit on page two beneath the headline, "Crash victim to sue candidate's daughter." Dad knew it was coming so he was not terribly upset or surprised. He was, however, pretty worried about Clarissa. She spent the night of the great debate at our house and has since moved into the guest room down the hall from me.

Rufus quit his job at *The Recorder* and joined our staff on election night. We all gathered in Kip's office when it was over. Rufus was an instant hit: he smoked, he drank, and the only time he looked even a wee bit uncomfortable was when Dixie asked him what type of underwear he was wearing.

"What do you mean?" said Rufus, with a nervous little smile on his face.

"I mean, what kind of underwear are you wearing?" said Dixie, putting down her drink temporarily and looking right at him.

Rufus looked to me for help, but I just shrugged my shoulders. He looked at Tom, and Tom raised his eyebrows, as if to say that he too was interested, and offered him a mini-carrot.

"I'm wearing boxers," said Rufus, after a moment.

"How do they fit?" said Tom.

"Any pictures on them?" said Kip.

Rufus looked like he wanted to escape through a hole in the floor. "They fit fine," he said.

"No uncomfortable creeping or anything like that?" said Dixie, retrieving her cup.

"No," said Rufus.

Dixie nodded. "Good," she said. "Just checking."

"You know what I was thinking," said Kip, leaning back in his chair. He was thoroughly enjoying the night. "I was thinking about those bras that Harper's girlfriend was looking at."

"She wasn't actually looking at them," I said, feeling a need to set the record straight.

"No, but I bet you were," said Dixie.

"No, I wasn't," I said, turning red. I had brought my own can of pop in for the night's celebration, so I wasn't nearly as vocal as I had been the time before.

"Why, don't they come in a box?" said Dixie.

"Of course they do," said Tom.

"I haven't been looking at anything," I said, which was the truth.

"I was thinking about that," said Kip, returning us to his point, "and I thought to myself, 'You know what? They should make liquid-lift underwear for guys.'"

Dixie nearly spit her drink out of her mouth when he said that.

"I'm serious," said Kip. "Why not?"

"Maybe they do," said Tom.

"I've never heard of them," said Kip.

"I've never heard of them," said Dixie.

"I think I read something once," said Tom.

"I don't know," said Kip. He looked over at Rufus and me. "Which one of you two wants to look into it? Maybe there's a story there we could run someday when the news is slow."

"I say Rufus," said Dixie. "He's the new kid."

"I say Harper," said Tom. "You could do kind of a his and her thing with his girlfriend. Like that movie, *He Said, She Said*."

Kip thought for a moment. "I never saw that one."

"It wasn't very good," said Dixie.

"I liked it," said Tom.

"It wasn't very good," said Dixie, looking at Kip.

"You take it, Rufus," said Kip, making his decision based on who-knows-what. " We'll give Harper the day off. He can go shopping instead."

"He can go browsing," said Dixie, laughing.

I finished my pop a short time later and hit the road.

I had not written a column for the week leading up to the election because Kip needed the space for ads, so I went home and wrote one for the next issue of the paper.

I was not sure what I would write about when I first sat down, but as things have been going lately, with regards to writing, anyway, the words just started coming and I just typed them onto the page.

It went like this:

This is the first job I have ever had in my life.

If it was a first date, I think we would have turned to each other long before the movie even started and said, "I really don't think this is going to work," and we would have left the theater and gone our separate ways, one of us carrying the popcorn, the other one carrying the pop.

If it was a puppy dog I had just brought home, I think I would have sat down with it on the floor in the kitchen and said, "You know what, Fred?" (I have always wanted to have a dog named Fred.) "I think you'd be better off in a different home. I don't think this is the best home for you. Let's go find you somewhere else to live. Somewhere that will really make you happy."

But it's not. It's my first job, as I said, and it's arranged through school yet, so I can't exactly quit it, unless I want to lose my credits, which would only make things worse.

I am sure most of you already know about my trials as a court reporter, which are small compared to the trials facing another person I know, but still, in my little life, they are big.

I have never snitched on anyone before, but that

is how I felt when I wrote the story about my sister.

Was it really a snitch though? I don't know. I doubt it, actually. But it was certainly one of those things that a lot of people would rather not have known about, including myself.

My sister has always been a bit of a mysterious person in my life. She was not around much when I was little, and when she was, it wasn't to play with me.

She moved away when I was young and I didn't miss her for a minute. To me, she was someone I knew as "my sister" and that was it. If anyone wanted to know anything more about her, or anything about her at all, they would have been directed by me to Mom and Dad.

What I have learned about her lately is not what I was looking for. If nothing else, my sister has always stood for the meaning of success: although she wasn't exactly the sweetest person I'd ever met, she was a fine example of what a little hard work and commitment could get you.

Now I look at her and think that this "Life" business is a pretty tough thing to manage, and if she can't do it, what on earth makes me think that I can?

As a person graduating from high school next year, I can think of a few other things that I would rather have on my mind, but a little cloudburst of reality over your head is not the worst thing in the world, so long as you don't settle in to be wet for the rest of your life.

I know Clarissa won't be. She will rise to her feet and live her life again, and so will Mom and Dad.

As for me, I am just starting, and I'm learning as I go along, with my eyes open, as a good reporter should, meaning, I guess, that I shouldn't be too hasty to write this first job off.

Maybe, just maybe, my date in the movie theater would turn to me and say, "Hey, good pick. I think I'm going to like going out with you."

Wouldn't that be a fun way to start things off?

I dropped the column off with Kip and he told me later that he liked it. Then he told me that even though the election was over, I may as well keep writing it, since he could use a little time off.

I was happy to hear that.

Don Trembath was born in Winnipeg, Manitoba, and moved to Alberta at the age of fourteen. He graduated from the University of Alberta in 1988, with a BA in English.

Don's first novel, *The Tuesday Cafe*, was inspired by six years of work at the Prospects Literary Association in Edmonton. It was nominated for both the Young Adult Library Services Association Best Books for Young Adults and the YALSA Quick Picks for Reluctant Readers lists. It also won the R. Ross Annett Award for Children's Literature and made the ALA's "Popular Paperbacks" 1997 list. The second installment in the Harper Winslow series, *A Fly Named Alfred*, was nominated for the prestigious Mr. Christie's Book Award. *A Beautiful Place on Yonge Street* was chosen as a YALSA Popular Paperbacks for Young Adults.

Lefty Carmichael Has A Fit, Don's fourth book, was nominated for the Canadian Library Association Young Adult Book Award and has been widely praised by such journals as *Publishers Weekly*, *School Library Journal,* and *Booklist*. It was also included in the YALSA "Best Books for Young Adults," for the year 2001.

Don divides his time between school and library presentations and his active young family.

Also in the Harper Winslow Series

THE TUESDAY CAFE

* ALA Best Book nominee
* PNLA Young Readers Choice finalist
* YALSA Popular Paperbacks for Young Adults
* Alberta Book Award

It all started with a small fire in a garbage can. Unfortunately, the garbage can was in the hallway of Harper's school …

Harper Winslow has some problems. His parents don't seem to understand what is going on in his life at all. He's not doing well at school. And a juvenile court judge has just ordered him to write a 2000-word essay on how he is going to turn his life around.

Now his mother has enrolled him in a writing class called The Tuesday Cafe, but it's not the kind of class she expected.

1-55143-074-6, Can $8.95 / US $6.95
Accelerated Quiz # 18600

Also in the Harper Winslow Series

A FLY NAMED ALFRED

* ALA Quick Picks for Reluctant YA Readers nominee
* Mr. Christie's Book Award finalist

Harper Winslow is in trouble.

"Alfred" (a pseudonym) writes a column called *Fly on the Wall* for the school newspaper. The column is a big hit with students. Harper thinks this is great. Or at least he does until Alfred pokes fun at a local thug, who then puts a bounty on the head of the columnist.

Things begin to get complicated when a school bully decides that Harper should be the one to find out who Alfred really is. If Harper reveals what he knows, he'll be in big trouble!

A Fly Named Alfred is Don Trembath's second novel. His first, The Tuesday Cafe, also deals with the turbulent life of Harper Winslow.

1-55143-083-5, Can $8.95 / US $6.95
Accelerated Quiz #20459

Also in the Harper Winslow Series

A BEAUTIFUL PLACE ON YONGE STREET

* YALSA Popular Paperbacks for Young Adults nominee
* Starred review Booklist

Harper Winslow is in love.

Sunny Taylor is tall and thin, with the smoothest, whitest skin Harper has ever seen. Her eyes are deep and dark, her voice a little high and sweet. And she is an artist.

For the moment, at least, life is full of smiles and love. But hovering above all of this brightness, like a thundercloud on a hot summer day, is a decision that Sunny must make. Will she stay in Edmonton or will she move to Toronto to live with her aunt and attend art school? And will Harper survive his first brush with the vagaries of love?

A Beautiful Place on Yonge Street is the third installment in the adventures of Harper Winslow.

"... non-stop, intense wit and commentary ... a fine conclusion. " – *Booklist*

"... beautifully written ..." – *Resource Links*

1-55143-121-1, Can $7.95 / US $6.95
Accelerated Quiz #27525

More teen fiction

LEFTY CARMICHAEL HAS A FIT

* ALA Best Book nominee
* YALSA Popular Paperbacks for Young Adults nominee

When fifteen-year-old Lefty Carmichael finds out he has epilepsy, his world is turned upside down. The idea of having a seizure at a totally unexpected moment is pretty scary at first, but Lefty comes to believe that he can handle it. What he's not sure he can handle is the reaction of his family and friends to the news of his disability. His mom passes out the first time she witnesses a seizure. His best friend Rueben spreads rumors about him. His almost-girlfriend is too scared to be alone with him anymore. And it gets worse!

1-55143-166-1, Can $7.95 / US $6.95
Accelerated Reader Quiz #36035